Praise for

THE BLUEBELL GADSBY SERIES

'Raucously funny.'
New York Times

'Ebullient, life-affirming, witty.'
Lovereading

'Funny and po[...]heart.'

'Hugely recommended [...] astute...
[...]arming.'
YA Yeah Yeah
Book Trust

'Quirky and hugely entertaining.'
Children's Bookseller's Choice

'Sweet, funny, heart-warming – just plain wonderful.'
So Many Books, So Little Time

'Memorable – funny, tumultuous.'
Wall Street Journal

'Everything I wanted it to be.'
Luna's Little Library

'Natasha Farrant is exceptional at capturing the details of family life and the swirling [...] surr[...]
Julia Eccle[...]

'Funny and moving – a classic portrait of a family just [...]h to be [...]g.'
[...]*aph*

FABER & FABER

has published children's books since 1929. Some of our very first publications included *Old Possum's Book of Practical Cats* by T. S. Eliot, starring the now world-famous Macavity, and *The Iron Man* by Ted Hughes. Our catalogue at the time said that 'it is by reading such books that children learn the difference between the shoddy and the genuine'. We still believe in the power of reading to transform children's lives.

ABOUT THE AUTHOR

Natasha Farrant has worked in children's publishing for almost twenty years, running her own literary scouting agency for the past ten. She is the author of the Carnegie-longlisted and Branford Boase-shortlisted YA historical novel *The Things We Did For Love*, as well as two successful adult novels. Natasha was shortlisted for the Queen of Teen Award 2014, and the second Bluebell Gadsby book, *Flora in Love*, was longlisted for the Guardian Children's Fiction Prize.

She grew up in London where she still lives with her husband, their two daughters and a large, tortoiseshell cat. She is the eldest of four siblings and would still like to have her own pony.

ALL ABOUT PUMPKIN

Natasha Farrant

FABER & FABER

First published in 2015
by Faber & Faber Limited
Bloomsbury House,
74–77 Great Russell Street,
London WC1B 3DA

Typeset by MRules

Printed by CPI Group (UK) Ltd, Croydon CRO 4YY

The right of Natasha Farrant to be identified as
author of this work has been asserted in accordance with
Section 77 of the Copyright, Designs and Patents Act 1988

A CIP record for this book
is available from the British Library

ISBN 978–0–571–29799–3

FSC
www.fsc.org
MIX
Paper from
responsible sources
FSC® C101712

2 4 6 8 10 9 7 5 3 1

For Alice, Elfie and Holly

Being a combination of conventional diary entries and transcripts of short films shot by the author on the camera she was given for her thirteenth birthday, beginning at the end of summer.

The Film Diaries of Bluebell Gadsby

Scene One
Arrival

Plumpton railway station. A single
track, an old stone platform, a bench,
a low white building housing a ticket
office (empty), toilets (closed), a café/
newspaper/sweetshop (also closed). On
the railway side, overgrown hedgerows
bursting with cow parsley and brambles.
On the Plumpton side, a road stretching
one way into town, the other out
towards the Devon countryside. The
car park, mostly made of potholes, is
empty. The whole scene bakes in the
afternoon sun.

Two children sit in the shade of
the station building. JASMINE (ten
years old, long tangled black hair,

sparkly flip-flops, not very clean dress) sits on top of her suitcase, eating chocolate biscuits and scowling. TWIG (twelve years old, skinny, brown hair flopping into his eyes) sits on the floor, reading Victor Hugo's one-thousand-three-hundred-and-seventy-six-page novel *Les Misérables*. He mouths the words as his eyes follow them across the page. Their sister BLUEBELL (aka CAMERAMAN, fourteen) is off picture behind the camera she uses to record her family. She wears denim cut-offs, a purple T-shirt, faded green sneakers and tortoiseshell glasses. Her long brown hair hangs past her shoulders in two neat braids.

They are waiting for their grandmother.

JASMINE, to CAMERAMAN
Try calling her again.

CAMERAMAN (BLUEBELL)
I told you, there's no signal.
There's never any signal here. She's
probably just stuck in traffic.

                    TWIG

          She's *over an hour* late.

                  JASMINE

    What if she *never* gets here? What if
     she's had an accident and died?

                    TWIG

       We'd get the next train home.

                  JASMINE
                (ignores him)
    What would happen to us without
    a telephone? We'd be stuck here
                  for ever!

                 CAMERAMAN
      (sounding a little disapproving)
    If Grandma died it would also be
              very, *very* sad.

                    TWIG

    And a little bit our fault, seeing as
    she was driving here to pick us up.

                      3

                          JASMINE

    But I don't even *want* to be here!

Jasmine's wails are cut short by the
sound of an approaching engine. Camera
turns to entrance of the car park. A
Land Rover (the really old kind like
you sometimes see in films) bounces
towards them across the potholes, and
stalls in front of them. Grandma waves
cheerily out of the window.

It was meant to be the four of us and Mum coming to Devon in the car, but then Twig dropped the baby on his head.

He was just trying to pick Pumpkin up from his cot because he was crying, but Pumpkin is really wriggly. It wasn't a big drop. He only bounced a tiny bit on his mattress, but he howled for ages, it was five o'clock in the morning and Mum was even more tired than usual because Zoran and Gloria came for supper before he went to Bosnia to visit his sister, and they stayed for ages.

'I was trying to help,' Twig explained when Mum staggered into Pumpkin's room to see what all the noise was, but she told him to just go back to bed.

'I have had the most shocking night,' she told Grandma on the phone this morning. 'I am thoroughly exhausted and it's not safe for me to drive. I'm afraid we shan't be able to set out until I've had a nap.'

Grandma, who is often quite tactless and who shouts so loudly on the phone that everyone can hear her, yelled 'REALLY, CASSIE, I SHOULD HAVE THOUGHT THAT AFTER SIX BABIES YOU WOULD BE ABLE TO COPE!' and Mum hung up and called Dad on his film set in New Zealand.

'We're about to start shooting,' he told her.

'I don't care,' she said.

She waved us out of the room. We tried listening at the door but we couldn't hear anything except for when Mum shouted, 'Why do you think I'm tired, David, I'm looking after four children single-handed; one never sleeps more than two hours at a time and the others are trying to kill him!'

Jas and I looked at Twig.

'I was trying to *help*,' he repeated.

'I don't care if it's too much for your mother since her fall,' Mum was yelling. 'If she can't cope with three responsible children without me there, then they can stay here. I can't look after an old lady, three kids and a baby.'

'Is Grandma the old lady?' Twig whispered.

'I suppose so,' I said.

'And are we the responsible children?'

'You're not,' Jas said. 'You're a baby dropper.'

'Shh,' I said. 'I think Mum's crying.'

And then we all jumped up and pretended to be very busy on the landing as Mum came out of her room, sniffing a little bit and saying that if we hurried, we just had time to catch the 10.46 from Paddington.

'I thought we were driving,' Twig said.

6

'I'm not coming to Devon.' Mum couldn't quite look at us as she said that, but I could see her eyes were red. 'I'm sorry. It's just for a little bit.'

'But what about Pumpkin?' Jas cried.

'Also staying in London with me.' Mum smiled, the way people do when they really hope you're not going to make a fuss.

'For how long?' Twig asked.

'A couple of weeks.' She still couldn't look at us. 'Maybe three? I'm sorry, darlings. Just think of it like any other year. You always go to Grandma's on your own.'

'This is my first summer holiday with a baby brother,' Jas declared. 'If Pumpkin's staying, so am I.'

Mum closed her eyes and said very calmly, 'You are all going to Devon.'

Jas complained all the way to Paddington, but it didn't change a thing, not even when she started to cry.

'Be good for your grandmother,' Mum said. 'And I'll see you soon.'

It's not true that we always come to Devon on our own. Before Iris died, Mum and Dad always used to come too. This was supposed to be the year when Mum finally came with us again, and she was going to stay all summer because she's on maternity leave until September.

She looked relieved as the train pulled out of the station. We all saw it. The train doors closed, and she held Pumpkin up and waved his little hand at us, and then her whole body relaxed as she buried her face in his neck.

'Your fault,' Jas snapped at Twig.

'IT WAS AN ACCIDENT!' he roared.

'Please shut up,' I said.

'You can't talk to us like that,' Jas informed me.

'I can, because I'm the oldest.'

'You are *not* the oldest,' Twig pointed out.

'I am for as long as Flora's with Dad in New Zealand,' I said, and everyone sulked.

Grandma's Land Rover has room for three in the front, with two benches facing each other in the back. It used to be blue, but over the years it's faded to a sort of dark grey. The engine makes a rattling noise like it's dying, you can't lock the doors and there's a hole in the roof, but Grandma loves it. Years ago, when she and Grandpa still had dogs and sometimes sheep, they put a dog guard separating the front from the back, and they never took it away. The result is that anyone who goes in the back always ends up feeling like they should really be an animal, especially as Grandma has never bothered to clean it up. There are still dog blankets all over the floor, and a stainless steel water bowl, at least four leads and quite a lot of straw.

When we were little, we used to curl up on the floor and pretend to be puppies.

'Get in, get in!' Grandma cried. 'The sun is shining and the garden awaits!'

'You're late,' Jas informed her, climbing into the back.

'Only a few minutes!' she carolled.

'Over an *hour*.'

'SHALL WE GO CROSS COUNTRY?' Grandma didn't wait for an answer, but veered suddenly off the road onto a farm track.

Bowling across the countryside with the windows wide open, hedgerows bursting with flowers, the bright blue sky above and the wind whipping through my hair, I almost forgot about everything – Mum not coming, and Pumpkin, and Iris. The track came to an end and we were back on the single-track road across the moor. The landscape opened up, the moor spread out on either side as far as we could see, and despite everything I felt a bubble of excitement at being here. I peered through the dog guard into the back. Jas was still sulking. Twig was hanging on to a hand strap with his eyes closed and his face turned into the wind.

'Woof,' I said. Twig opened his eyes and smiled.

'Woof woof,' he replied.

And then we turned off the road onto the private lane down to Horsehill. The trees thickened as we came off the moor, and the lane became less tarmac and more grass and moss, and we were driving through the old white gate into the gravel courtyard and there was the house, all grey stone and big windows, and we were here.

'Home!' Grandma stalled again and pulled on the handbrake. She clambered down from the Land Rover and reached under her seat for a walking stick.

'Since when do you use that?' I asked.

'Just get those cases into the house,' she said, and hobbled away from the car.

'Why's she walking like that?' Jas asked.

'She had that fall.' I frowned, remembering. 'Right after Pumpkin was born. It was raining and she slipped. Mum was upset because Dad spent all the Easter holidays shuttling between London and here.'

'But that was ages ago,' Jas said.

'She seems OK now,' Twig observed.

Grandma was standing at the front door, waving her stick at us.

'I MADE CHOCOLATE CAKE!' she bellowed. 'And it's not going to eat itself!'

Mum always used to say that Iris was always most herself when she was here, because she was free to do everything she loved most, climbing and exploring and running about. On the first night of every holiday, she used to lie in the bed next to mine and plan everything we were going to do. Even after she died, I would still lie in bed every first night, thinking about all the things I was going to do, the same things I did with her, like our favourite walks and eating raspberries straight from the bush and lying in the stream with our heads under water. That's the thing about having a twin sister. It's been four years since she was hit by that van, but in my head, she's always with me.

I was planning not to come this year. Dodi invited me to go to Spain with her family, to her parents' villa in the south where they go every summer. 'We'll spend all our time at the beach,' she said, 'and we'll get you a tan and a new haircut and nice clothes and find you a boyfriend. Now that I'm going out with Jake, you have to have one too.'

Even though I've told her a million times that

I'm really happy for her and she's still my best friend, Dodi still feels awkward about the fact that she's going out with Jake because I went out with him first. She never listens when I tell her I don't even *want* a boyfriend, but I don't – not one like Jake anyway, who is lovely but a bit hopeless. One day, I want to fall in love like Flora did with Zach – totally, completely, absolutely. I want a soul mate – like Iris, though different, obviously. Otherwise I'm not really interested.

I did want to go to Spain though, because I thought it would be nice to go somewhere with no sad memories, and also fun to be with Dodi and swim in the Mediterranean Sea and reinvent myself as a glamorous, suntanned, sophisticated person, but Dad said no because Grandma would be disappointed.

'Grandma would totally understand,' I argued. 'She loves travelling. She's always zooming around the world doing exciting things.'

'She would be disappointed,' he repeated. 'And besides . . .'

'Besides what?'

But he wouldn't say.

So I'm in bed now, trying to hold on to the excitement I felt in the car. The night's still warm and the window's wide open, and outside I can hear all the sounds of the countryside at night – animals hunting, a car far away, the stream rushing by under the bridge. Horsehill is exactly the same as it is every summer. The house is big and friendly and smells of wood smoke and Grandma's cooking. Apples and plums are starting to grow on the trees, the kitchen garden is full of carrots and lettuces and tomatoes. Marigold and Hester, the fat old ponies, are dozing in the paddock, roses are climbing all over the walls and a few fields away the moor is sitting purple and green, waiting for us. Before coming to bed, I said goodnight to Jas and Twig in the room they always sleep in, with the same night light on because Twig doesn't like the dark. I have the same white bedspread over the same green and pink flowered duvet cover.

If Zoran were still our nanny and not an aspiring musician going out with a glamorous riding instructress, maybe Mum wouldn't be so tired. Maybe he would be here with us, and she would have come too, with Pumpkin. And if Flora were here, the room would be a mess. There would be clothes all over the floor, and empty mugs and glasses and chocolate wrappers on the table. She'd be sitting up in bed listening to music and complaining about there being no Wi-Fi or mobile reception and how she didn't know how she was expected to survive without hearing from Zach every five minutes and how no one understands what it's like to be in love.

But Flora isn't here. She is in New Zealand with Dad, playing a tiny part in the film he wrote about King Arthur, and we are here for the first time without her, Zoran is in Sarajevo and Grandma has a stick and Mum is staying in London with our four-month-old baby brother.

Everything feels different this year.

The Film Diaries of Bluebell Gadsby

Scene Two
The Mysterious Appearance of Two Boys in the Paddock

Morning. CAMERAMAN (BLUE) stands at the open window of her top-floor bedroom at Horsehill, filming. It is only eight o'clock, but already the air is hazy with heat. Birds sing. The stream gurgles. Everything is very, very pretty, but this is not what the camera focuses on.

There is a strange car parked in the courtyard below. It is strange for many different reasons. Firstly, it doesn't belong to Grandma. Secondly, it's a convertible, old-looking, with a dark grey body, huge headlights and faded red leather seats and quite a large dent in the side. And thirdly, it has the steering wheel on the left-hand side, meaning it's not English.

Off camera, the sound of the bedroom door creaking open. TWIG and JAS come to stand beside Cameraman, dressed respectively in way too short pyjamas and a torn floor-length lace-trimmed nightie.

                    TWIG
          (displaying dazzling boyish
                 knowledge)
Wow! A vintage Citroen DS convertible with a French number plate!

                    JAS
        (getting straight to the point)
             Whose is it?

A WOMAN appears around the side of the house. She carries an empty shopping crate, with a woven straw shopping basket hanging from her wrist. Children (and camera) lean forward for a better look. The woman looks about

the same age as their mother (forty
and a bit) but she is dressed like a
much younger hippy (Cameraman thinks),
in indigo harem pants, leather flip-
flops and a flowing purple vest top.
She is small and slight, with dark
curly hair streaked with grey hanging
down to her waist and kept off her
face with a bright green bandana. Her
wrists are heavy with silver bangles.

JAS
(confused)
Who is she?

The Nameless Woman throws basket and
shopping crate into the car then,
shading her eyes, turns towards the
paddock. She shouts something, waving.
Camera turns, following her gaze.

Two people sit on the fence around
the paddock, about a hundred metres
away from the house. Camera zooms
in. They are boys, one tall and fair,
the other smaller with darker hair.
A small black and white dog lies at

their feet. The smaller boy calls out to the ponies (MARIGOLD and FAT HESTER), who trot towards him like he is their best friend. He holds out his hand. They nuzzle it, looking for food. He pats them and kisses them on the nose. Then he grabs the halter of the larger pony (Marigold) and slips off the fence on to her bare back. The fair boy calls out after him, but he doesn't answer. He and Marigold are off, cantering around the paddock.

JAS
(awestruck)
And who is *he*?

The Nameless Woman was in the kitchen when we came down, making porridge, and she introduced herself straight away. Her name is Lizzie Hanratty and she is Grandma's closest neighbour, ever since she and her son Skye (the smaller boy) moved to the old cottage half a mile away at the beginning of last term. They used to live in France (hence the car), Skye's father is an artist and is still teaching there at some artist summer camp, and goodness there's a lot to do when you move into a new house.

'Skye's out with the ponies right now,' she told us. 'He comes every day, just to check them over. You'll meet him later. His cousin Ollie is staying with us for the summer, which is wonderful company for Skye and also so helpful, with all the painting and redecorating and repairing and everything. The boys are the same age as you, Bluebell. I hope you will all be wonderful, wonderful, wonderful friends.'

Lizzie Hanratty talks a *lot*.

'Normally they come on their bikes,' she said. 'But I just popped over with them this morning to bring a bit of shopping and I thought while I'm here, I might get on with making a bit of breakfast. Help yourselves to toast while I get on with the porridge. There's some of my homemade marmalade on the table. I've been helping Granny out a bit, you know, since she had her little fall. Such a shame your mum and the little one couldn't make it, but how lovely for Granny to have you for such a nice long holiday.'

Jas said, 'Twig dropped the baby on his head.'

Lizzie said wasn't that unfortunate and she hoped the baby was all right and she was sure it was just an accident.

'It was,' Twig mumbled.

'Mum's just tired,' I said. 'And the baby's fine.'

Lizzie said weren't my parents lucky to have a nice sensible daughter like me.

'Blue hates it when people call her sensible,' Jas said. She peered over the edge of Lizzie's saucepan. 'And it's way too hot for porridge.'

Then Grandma came in, looking annoyed.

'Really Lizzie, I am perfectly capable of making breakfast for my grandchildren. I'm not a complete invalid.' Jas sidled up to her and whispered in her ear. Grandma whispered back, loudly, that SHE HATES PORRIDGE TOO.

I felt quite sorry for Lizzie Hanratty.

The garden door burst open and the dog shot in, followed by the boys.

Skye Hanratty is the messiest-looking person I have ever seen. His hair is the colour of wet sand and it stands up all over his head in little tufts, like he tried to cut it himself and then gave up halfway through. His eyes are sort of sludge-coloured and he wears little wire-rimmed glasses held together with sticking plasters, he has a gap between his front teeth and freckles all over his face, there is dried mud on his jodhpurs, his torn T-shirt is covered in grass stains and the laces of his trainers are undone. He tore into the kitchen, saw us and stopped so suddenly his cousin, who was behind, crashed right into him.

'Sorry,' Skye said. 'The dog . . .'

The dog's name is Elsie, she belongs to Skye and she is mostly, but not completely, a border collie. She's very young, almost a puppy, and doesn't do any of the things she's told. He ordered her to sit but instead she ran three times round the kitchen, stuck her nose between everybody's legs, barked, tried to catch her own tail, then jumped up and pawed at Grandma, who kissed her on the nose, which made her so happy she finally stopped moving and rolled onto her back, with her pink tongue lolling out of the side of her mouth like she was smiling.

'Deal with her, Skye,' Lizzie murmured.

Skye dived forward to grab Elsie by the collar, tripped on his shoelaces, knocked into the corner of the table and sent Lizzie's homemade marmalade flying. Ollie, who has golden hair and blue eyes and clean clothes and very straight teeth, caught it just before it hit the ground and put it back on the table.

'Just sit down,' he said. 'And don't move.'

Skye dropped onto a chair. Elsie put her chin on his thigh and gazed at him. He scratched her ears with one hand, and rubbed the other over his face, leaving a smudge of dust across his nose.

'I'm trying to train her,' he said, looking up at us.

'Dogs will be dogs,' Grandma said.

'Your granny's amazing,' Lizzie said, and Grandma flinched. She hates being called Granny.

Skye was busy trying to teach Elsie to stay sitting by pressing down her bottom and wagging his finger in her face. Lizzie nudged him and nodded at us.

'What?' he asked.

'Introduce yourself,' she whispered.

Ollie sighed and stepped forward, taking a low, theatrical bow.

'Ladies,' he said, flourishing an imaginary hat

at Jas and me, then turned to Twig. 'Sir. Oliver Blackerry, at your most distinguished service.'

Flora would have curtseyed right back and simpered something like 'Oh sir, you are too kind.'

Twig and Jas and I just stared.

Close up and smiling, Oliver Blackerry is *spectacularly* good-looking.

'Now you tell me your names,' he said kindly.

'Bluebell,' I managed. 'And this is Twig, and this is Jas.'

'Skye?' Lizzie prompted.

He gave a little wave, like he was apologising for not being as flamboyant as his cousin.

'I'm Skye,' he said.

'That's Skye with an "e" at the end,' Lizzie explained. 'As in the Scottish island. Not the actual sky. It's where he was conceived.'

Ollie snorted with laughter. No one else knew quite what to say. Skye rolled his eyes, like he was used to this story and it had lost the power to embarrass him, but then Jas, who hadn't said anything until now, burst out with 'We saw you riding, and you looked amazing!' and he blushed.

'I love riding,' Jas told him. 'We have an ex-nanny called Zoran and his girlfriend, her name's Gloria, has these riding stables in London, and I ride there all the time. They're right under the motorway, nothing like here, but I'm really good. Will you teach me to ride without a saddle like you?'

'Sure.' Skye grinned, showing the gap in his teeth. Lizzie beamed.

'Only if Granny says yes!' she warned. 'Skye's a good teacher, aren't you, Skye? There's nothing he doesn't know about horses. We lived near a livery stables in France, and he was always squirrelled away there. The owners said they had never met anyone with such natural ability.'

Skye was so red now his freckles were almost invisible. Ollie pulled him to his feet and started to push him towards the door.

'Let's go,' he said. 'Before Skye actually catches fire.'

Lizzie made Grandma promise to call if she needed anything. 'Even the slightest, teeniest thing!' she said, and swept out to the car. Ollie bowed again. I got the feeling he was laughing at us a bit. Skye whistled to Elsie, bumped into the door, muttered 'Ow!' and stumbled out into the sunshine.

'Gosh,' I said.

'My new neighbours,' Grandma agreed.

'They're very . . .'

'What?'

And I really didn't know what to say. Gorgeous? Clumsy? Overwhelmingly friendly?

'Nice,' I said.

Grandma grunted and said that if we'd finished breakfast, she could use some help in the garden.

Mum called. Her old school friend Gaia, who got divorced last year and lives in a big peaceful house in the country near Basingstoke, has invited her and Pumpkin to stay for 'a nice long rest'.

'She can rest here,' Twig said while Jas was ordering Mum to come to Horsehill instead.

'Not really,' Grandma reasoned, with her usual tact. 'If you think about it. Not with you lot.'

Then Dad called later, when everyone except Jas was in the garden. I went in to answer but she was already talking to him.

'I don't *really* mind being here,' she was saying. 'Because there's this boy and the ponies. I just want Mummy and Pumpkin to be here too.' She kicked the skirting board while Dad replied. 'But I can look after Pumpkin if Mummy wants to rest,' she protested, and then 'Why are grown-ups always, *always* tired?'

There was a clunk as she put the phone down and shouted that Dad wanted to speak to me too. She hovered while I talked to him with her head pressed against mine. I tried to shove her away, but she said she wanted to hear what he had to say.

'How is she?' he asked.

'Jas?'

'Your grandmother. I don't want you tiring her out.'

Jas rolled her eyes. Grandma wandered in from the garden, brandishing her stick with one hand and a courgette with the other.

'Is that your father?'

I passed her the phone.

'You're fussing again,' she told him.

Dad said something I didn't hear. Grandma told him he was speaking nonsense and hung up.

The old family cot that we all slept in is out in the little box room next to where Mum and Dad always sleep. The white wood has faded to yellow, and some of the old cartoon characters painted on the sides are almost rubbed out, but someone had dusted and cleaned it, laid out crisply ironed baby sheets and a little cotton blanket, and put Dad's old teddy bear out on the chest of drawers.

Jas cried when she saw the room. Even I got a lump in my throat.

I know Grandma did everything she could think

of to make things nice for us this evening. She let Jas eat just pasta and cheese even though she doesn't think it's a proper meal, and she melted a whole box of Belgian chocolates someone had given her to pour over ice cream, and after dinner we walked down to the stream and threw sticks into the water to race them under the bridge, like we used to when we were little.

It only cheered us up a little bit.

The Film Diaries of Bluebell Gadsby

Scene Three
Plant Life

DAY. EXTERIOR.

The kitchen garden at Horsehill (referred to by GRANDMA as the 'potager') measures exactly eighteen feet by twelve and faces full south, sheltered on one side by the wall of the garden and on the other by the house.

In this unusually hot summer, after a damp spring (ideal growing conditions, according to Grandma), the kitchen garden explodes with produce. French and runner beans twist around bamboo wigwams. Their scarlet flowers sway in the breeze, as do the feathery tops of rows and rows of carrots. Black and redcurrant bushes droop with heavy fruit. Courgette flowers bloom orange and yellow, their snaking vines threatening to invade onion beds overgrown with weeds. Camera zooms in on one courgette, swollen to the size of a marrow and beginning to split. Bees hum among the flowers of inedible lettuce heads gone to seed.

Grandma, straight and tiny, long grey hair tied back in its usual bun, pearl earrings in place, dressed in ancient gardening clothes of nondescript colour, wide-brimmed straw hat and bright purple Crocs, marches up and down the rows of vegetables followed by TWIG and JASMINE, both wearing expressions of mounting dismay as she issues the day's instructions, jabbing at beds with her walking stick.

GRANDMA

Pick all the French beans longer
than twelve centimetres. Weed the
onion beds. Pick the courgettes.
Throw that marrow on the compost
heap. Check the size of the carrot
heads. If they're big enough,
pull them up.

TWIG

How do we know when they're
big enough?

Grandma makes a small circle with
her thumb and index finger to
indicate the optimum circumference
of a carrot head.

GRANDMA

Currants – if they are ripe, pick
them. Stick them in the freezer for
when we're ready to make jam. Ditto
raspberries – it's a new variety,
they should yield for another couple
of weeks. Don't put them in the
freezer, we'll have them for lunch.

JASMINE

I don't understand why you don't just
buy your vegetables from a shop.

GRANDMA
(looks appalled)
Why on earth would I do that? Come
along now, chop chop. Plants won't
look after themselves!

TWIG
Actually, Nature is full of plants
looking after themselves.

GRANDMA
(a little hurt)
You used to love helping
in the potager.

CAMERAMAN
(focusing on Twig)
We still do. Don't we, Twig?

TWIG
(mumbles)
Yes, we do.

JASMINE

(to Grandma)

What are you going to do while
we do all the work?

GRANDMA

(looks offended)

I am going to look after you.

We worked all afternoon. We cut and we hacked and pruned and tied and dug and weeded as Grandma instructed, but even though we have always helped in the garden I couldn't shake off the sense that things are not the same. Maybe it's the fact that usually when we come, Grandma is ready with a list of things for us to do – fun things as well as chores, like beach trips and picnics, bonfires, hikes. She's not mentioned anything like that yet. Or maybe it's the heat, or the fact that instead of bustling around as usual while we work, she fell asleep in a deckchair in the shade all afternoon. Or maybe it's like I wrote before, that nothing is the same.

Once, just after he stopped being our nanny to become a music teacher, Zoran told me that there are certain unshakeable facts in life, and that the sooner you accepted them, the easier it got.

It was Flora's seventeenth birthday. She was having a party, and said I couldn't go.

'It is *not* a party for children,' Flora said.

'And I am not a child,' I complained to Zoran.

The unshakeable fact Zoran told me to accept was this: nothing will ever change the way your family sees you. Zoran is twenty-seven now but twenty years ago, when there was a war in his country, his parents put him and his big sister Lena on a boat to escape from Bosnia. She led him all the way through Italy and France to England to live with their great-aunt Alina, but even though they are both completely grown-up now, she still treats him like the little boy she had to look after all that time ago.

'Just as you all treat me like I am still your nanny,' he said.

'So Flora will always be the loud, bossy, oldest one,' I said. 'And Twig will be the curious, clever boy, and Jas will be the cute little one, and I will always be the boring one in the middle.'

'We are who we are in the eyes of our family,' Zoran said, in that prim way he sometimes has. 'And you are not boring,' he added, just a tiny bit too late.

Here is something I have learned over the last few months.

Things do change. All it takes is a baby.

The first time we saw him was in hospital. He was two hours old, asleep in this clear plastic crib that looked like a fish tank, wrapped in a blanket so all you could see was his little neck and face, and he was all wrinkled and a bit purple with this shock of pale orange hair, which makes him sound alarming but actually he was really, really sweet. Mum was lying in bed, looking pale and a bit astonished, like she had never had a baby before, and Dad was holding her hand and crying and saying 'a little boy, a little boy' like *he*'d never had a son before, and even though it was this huge, momentous occasion, it didn't feel like anything had majorly changed. Jas read out a poem she composed on the Tube ('Here we are on our way to the hospital, Shaken by the train, To see our new brother, Like no other, I wonder what will be his name'). Twig poked around the nappies and bottom cream and cotton wool and babygrows to see how everything worked. Flora cried, 'Imagine if people thought he was *my* baby!', then we spent ages arguing about his name, with Dad wanting something boyish like Jim or Chester and everyone else saying he should have a flower name. It was Mum who came up with William (for Sweet William, the flower), and Jas who came up with the nickname Pumpkin, because of his little round cheeks and orange hair.

I filmed everything. We were all completely, absolutely typically ourselves. It was only afterwards, going home, that I realised what was happening.

'Oh my god,' Flora said. 'I think compared to that I'm like, an *adult*.'

'I'm not the youngest any more,' Jas said.

Twig said, 'I'm not the only boy.'

I thought, 'I just want my sister back.'

When she was pregnant, Mum said that no baby could ever replace Iris, but I saw the way she looked at Pumpkin in hospital. I've looked at my film of that day over and over again. She's gazing at him like he's the most amazing thing ever, and since then she has hardly ever let him out of her sight. It's all feeding Pumpkin, and burping Pumpkin, and how much is Pumpkin sleeping and Pumpkin's routine and 'Was that a smile, or does he just have wind?' It's not his fault. He's only a baby. All he really does is eat and sleep, but he has completely taken over our lives. I've tried hard over the past four months to see him as Mum does. It's not easy to get very close to him because Mum and Jas are so obsessed with him. I watch over him when they're out, and I push his buggy and rock him to sleep, and I've bounced him and cuddled him a few times, and all the time I have been waiting for Mum to talk to me and explain exactly how I am supposed to feel about all this, because I just don't know. But Mum is busy all the time. When she's not looking after Pumpkin, she's dealing with a drama of Flora's, or Dad with a writing deadline crisis, or Jas losing her homework or Twig doing stuff like putting his cricket mouthguard in the bottle steriliser. She doesn't have time for questions like mine.

For me, it boils down to this. I used to have a twin sister, but she died. I have a baby brother, who's alive. Somewhere between the two of them, there is a deep dark hole and I don't know how to fill it.

Tuesday 22 July

I haven't seen Skye and Ollie since that first day. They have been coming early when I'm still asleep, but Jas saw them this morning. I think she slept with an alarm clock under her pillow. She didn't think to wake anyone else up, but went straight down to the paddock without even getting dressed, to watch Skye exercise Marigold and Hester.

She came into my room afterwards to tell me all about it.

'Every day, he makes sure they have enough water, and he checks them for bites and ticks, and he clears their droppings out of the field so there aren't too many flies, and he makes sure there are no holes in the ground so they don't hurt themselves, and then he exercises them by riding them around. When he's got time, he takes them out on the moor. I'm longing to go out on the moor. I asked if I could I ride Hester without a saddle, because she's smaller than Marigold so if I fall it doesn't matter so much. And he was going to let me but then Ollie said weren't we supposed to ask Grandma, so I saddled her up and rode her *in my nightie*. It wasn't very comfortable. Dad says in King Arthur stories Lady Godiva rode around naked. Naked! Do you think Grandma *will* let Skye teach me to ride without a saddle?'

'Why don't you go and ask her now?'

'They've gone.' Jas looked suddenly deflated. 'They're painting a shed for Skye's father to do his art in. Well, Skye calls it a shed. Ollie says it's a studio. That's why they come so early.'

'I'm sure they'll be back tomorrow,' I said, but I felt a little deflated too.

Before she left for New Zealand, Flora's boyfriend Zach recorded this song for her that he wrote, all about how *There's a special star you see From every hemisphere However far apart we'll be When we watch it together We'll always be near.* No one had the heart to point out that this is physically impossible because it's always daytime in New Zealand when it's night in England and vice versa. The first thing Flora posted when she arrived was how she cried the entire flight to Auckland listening to it, but it looks like she's over all that now. She shot her first scene in Dad's film today. She has a tiny role playing a servant. She doesn't have any actual lines, but she didn't mention that. Instead it's all how she gets to wear an AWESOME medieval costume and WALK AROUND SWINGING A SWORD (because apparently that is what all medieval servants used to do) and the whole experience is AMAZING. She posted a photograph on Facebook looking all glowing and radiant, dressed in a sort of leather mini dress with mud all over her face and the caption 'I'm ready to be a film star!' underneath.

She called us this evening and told us to go on Skype so we could all talk to her together.

'So,' I asked once we were connected. 'Are you meeting lots of stars?'

'Heaps,' she said.

'Have you met Brandon Taylor yet?' Jas asked, and Flora replied airily that oh yes, she and Hollywood's biggest heartthrob hang out all the time, but meanwhile how was Devon, and was Grandma doing her usual thing of making us pick loads of vegetables and by the way were Zoran and Gloria engaged yet?

Flora is obsessed with other people's love lives.

'Zoran has gone to Sarajevo,' I reminded her, and she said that didn't mean he couldn't get engaged.

'There are two boys here,' said Jas.

'Now it's getting interesting,' Flora said.

'One lives in the old empty cottage, and the other's a cousin,' Jas said. 'They're both fourteen. The one who lives here is called Skye. He used to live in France, but they've come back for his education, because his mother wants him to go to an English school. His father's an artist and his mother wants to open a vegetarian café. She had one where they used to live in France, but it didn't do very well because the French like to eat meat. The other one is called Ollie. His parents are both lawyers. They live in Bath, but they're on holiday in Italy. They went without him but he doesn't mind because it's their wedding anniversary and like their second honeymoon. They're coming to visit soon. What?' she asked, because Twig and I were staring at her. 'I *told* you I'd spoken to them.'

'What else did they tell you?' I asked.

'Ollie's at boarding school and his parents are super rich. He does debating and school council and hockey and wants to go to Oxford. Skye goes to the comp in Plumpton and he hates school and doesn't like anyone in his year and wants to train race horses.'

'Never mind all that stuff,' Flora interrupted. 'Are they cute?'

'You're as bad as Dodi,' I said.

'Answer the question.'

'Skye has a dog,' Jas went on. 'She's a border collie mongrel cross. She's super cute.'

'Blue, how come Jas knows all about these boys and you don't?' Flora demanded. 'Have you even spoken to them yet? How are you ever going to get a boyfriend if you don't speak to boys?'

The nice thing about Flora being so far away is that you can just log off whenever she gets too much.

Wednesday 23 July

They came later today, in the car with Lizzie. I was still in bed, but awake this time. I heard them drive up, then voices, Lizzie shouting to be quick, the crunch of footsteps on gravel going round the house to the back door, Lizzie again calling hello. I kept thinking of Flora and all her questions, and it was awkward, because maybe everybody else was wondering the same, like why I hadn't spoken to them and was it because they were, well, boys. And I thought maybe I shouldn't go down at all but just stay in my room. But then my tummy rumbled, and I told myself if I didn't go down people would just wonder even more. So I waited a bit until I was sure the boys would be with the ponies so it wouldn't look like I went down specially to see them. I looked out of the window and sure enough, there was Skye cantering about on Marigold, but when I went into the kitchen there was Ollie was sitting at the table, eating toast heaped with Grandma's bramble jelly and trying to read Twig's copy of *Les Misérables*.

'Dude, you seriously like this stuff?' he was asking as I came in.

He closed the book and held it on his open palm, like he was weighing it. Twig said yes, he enjoyed it very much, but I think he was lying. He has been stuck on the same chapter since we got here. I'm pretty sure Jean Valjean hasn't even stolen the archbishop's silver yet.

'Heavy,' Ollie said, still weighing the book.

Lizzie said she thought it was wonderful that Twig liked reading.

'I write poetry,' Jas said, and Lizzie said that was even better, and that Skye loved reading too.

'Only books about horses and dog training.' Ollie dropped *Les Misérables* on the table. The thump made the tea in Grandma's cup slosh into her saucer. 'Dude, you should totally just watch the film.'

Grandma poured the tea from her saucer back into her cup and said with an edge in her voice that she thought the book was much better than the film, that she herself adored Victor Hugo and that when Twig finished *Les Misérables* she had his complete works in her bedroom for him to choose from.

Twig looked a bit uncertain and said, 'Thank you Grandma, I'll enjoy that too.'

'Bluebell!' Lizzie cried, like she'd only just noticed me. 'Would you mind awfully running down to the paddock to chivvy Skye? I'm taking the boys to the sea and I don't want to leave too late.'

'Can we go to the sea?' Jas asked.

'Not today,' Grandma said.

'When?'

Grandma said when it wasn't so hot. Jas said being hot was the whole point of going to the sea, and Grandma told her she'd think about it and meanwhile to go with me to fetch Skye.

'It's not fair,' Jas grumbled as we walked down together towards the paddock. 'How come they get to go to the beach and we don't? Plus at this rate I'm *never* going to get my lesson.'

'Don't pester Grandma,' I said.

'I'm not pestering!' Jas said indignantly. 'I'm *asking*. Oh look, there's Skye at the end of the paddock. And there's Elsie!'

The paddock at Horsehill is a couple of acres of meadow, with hawthorn hedges round two edges with a gated gap in the furthest side leading to another field, and a white picket fence around the other two sides. There's a rowan tree in the corner with a bench under it where the path from the house turns into a thicket of branches concealing the old stone barn where nobody goes any more. Hester was dozing under the tree on one side of the fence. Elsie lay in the grass on the other side, with her ears flat against her head, tied to a post at the end of a long red lead, whining.

Jas dropped to her knees and patted her head.

'Poor Elsie. I wonder why Skye tied her up. He didn't yesterday. She just ran around the paddock with him.'

'Look,' I said.

Skye was coming towards us on Marigold. He was riding bareback again, but today he was barefoot too, and he was crouched low over Marigold's neck with his knees drawn up like a jockey's. His gaze was fixed between her ears, and I've never seen anyone concentrate so hard. Jas waved, but I don't think he even realised we were there. He stayed like that for a few strides, then drew his legs up under him. Jas clapped her hands together.

'What's he doing?' I asked.

'He's kneeling,' she whispered.

'Why?'

A few more strides. Jas clutched my arm. Marigold's canter slowed, and suddenly Skye wasn't kneeling any more but crouching like a surfer, and then he wasn't crouching but actually standing, perfectly straight, with his arms to the side and the widest grin on his face.

He looked nothing like the clumsy boy in Grandma's kitchen, who crashed into furniture and couldn't find the right thing to say. He looked graceful, and agile, and – amazing.

Just watching him made me feel like I was flying.

Elsie barked, and the magic broke. Skye's eyes flickered towards the fence. He saw us standing there, lost concentration, fell to the ground and screamed.

'He's not getting up!' Jas cried. 'Blue, do something!'

I ran across the paddock. Skye lay on his back, his face deathly pale, tears of pain in his eyes.

'Can you move?' I asked. 'Just say yes or no. Can you wiggle your toes? Where does it hurt?'

Jas ran up behind me, saw Skye's tears and started to cry.

'Help me stand up,' Skye croaked.

I crouched down beside him. He put his right arm around my shoulders, and together we staggered to our feet.

'What's happened to your arm?' Jas gasped.

Skye was still leaning against me with his eyes closed, swaying a bit like he might be about to faint. I twisted round to look. His left arm was dangling like a puppet's.

'Run to the house,' I told Jas. 'Tell Lizzie to call an ambulance and then to come out here to help.'

'No!' Skye opened his eyes. 'Don't get Mum. Help me to the side.'

We walked very slowly to the edge of the paddock. Skye leaned against the fence and took a few deep breaths.

'You have to tug my arm,' he said.

'Excuse me?'

'I've dislocated my shoulder. When I tell you, tug my arm downwards, OK? Gentle, but firm. Now!'

I took his hand and tugged exactly like he told me. He did a weird, rotating shrug, there was a popping sound and then his arm wasn't dangling any more.

'All better,' he said, but he was still very pale.

Elsie was whining so hard she sounded like Pumpkin crying. Skye took a couple of steps towards her, then sank to sit cross-legged in the grass.

'I'll get her!' Jas ran off. I sat down in the grass opposite Skye.

'Are you sure you're OK?'

'Yeah.' His eyes were shut again and he was doing these long, deep breaths. Elsie bounced over, released by Jas, and lay with her head in his lap, licking his toes. He opened his eyes and smiled a bit shakily. 'It often happens when I fall off.'

'Do you fall off a lot?' I asked.

He shrugged, and winced. 'My glasses.'

Jas ran off again and found the glasses, quite a long way from where Skye fell. 'One of the lenses is broken,' she announced when she came back.

Skye groaned. 'Mum's going to kill me. I've only had these a month.'

'How will you see?' I asked.

'My right eye's OK.'

'It's the left lens that's broken.'

'That,' Skye sighed, 'is just typical.'

From the house, we heard the sound of Lizzie calling.

'Promise you won't tell her what happened,' he said.

'I think she ought to know.'

'No she oughtn't. I'm fine. Promise!'

'Fine,' I said. 'I promise. But she sent us to fetch you, and if you don't come now she's going to ask questions.'

We started to walk slowly up the path.

'Can you teach me to stand on a horse?' Jas asked.

'No, he can't!' They both turned to look at me, surprised. 'It's dangerous!'

'Not if you do it right,' Skye said.

'It was scary! That whole shoulder thing!'

'Oh, don't worry about that!' He was already starting to look a lot more cheerful.

'You're sounding sensible,' Jas warned me.

I flushed. 'Sensible doesn't have to mean boring.'

They both looked unconvinced.

'It doesn't,' I insisted. 'You don't have to nearly kill yourself to have fun.'

As we walked back to the house, Skye said to name one completely sensible thing that was also fun. Even paddling in the stream, he said, was potentially lethal.

'You could slip and twist your ankle. You could fall face first, hit your head on a rock, faint and drown.'

'You could choke eating chocolate cake,' Jas said.

'Is chocolate cake exciting?' Skye asked.

'It is quite exciting,' I admitted. He grinned, and almost fell over his feet.

'Hurry up!' Lizzie was standing by the car as we approached, with Ollie already in the front passenger seat. Skye hid his glasses behind his back. 'What took you so long? And Skye, where on earth are your shoes?'

'Oh God, my shoes!'

'I'll get them!' Jas started to run back towards the paddock, then turned back to Lizzie. 'He wasn't doing anything dangerous.'

Lizzie just said, 'Glasses?'

Skye grimaced and held them out.

'It's my fault!' I blurted.

Lizzie looked astonished. Ollie raised his eyebrows.

'He took them off to keep them safe,' I gabbled. 'And I trod on them.'

'You left your glasses on the ground?' Lizzie asked Skye.

'They were on the bench, but I . . . I stood on the bench.'

'Why?' asked Ollie.

'To get a better view of Skye riding.'

Ollie's eyebrows rose even further, but I think Lizzie believed us.

'They were already kind of broken anyway, Mum,' Skye offered.

'Well, get in the car then,' she sighed as Jas ran back. She didn't ask why Skye wasn't wearing his shoes.

He tried not to wince as he slid into the back of the car. 'Thank you,' he mouthed.

'You're welcome,' I mouthed back.

Ollie's eyebrows almost disappeared into his hair. Skye sank back into his seat, Lizzie tooted the horn and they were gone.

Here's another everyday thing that turned out to be dangerous: crossing the road. It was dark, and she probably wasn't looking – Iris never looked – but it was at a proper crossing place, the one we always used for school.

About three years after Iris died, Jake taught me how to skateboard. And one evening, when I was feeling really sad and angry, I went to the park with him after dark, and told him I wanted to fly. I spent ages going backwards and forwards up and down a ramp, higher and higher until I managed to do a flip. I fell and everything hurt afterwards but it was the sort of thing she would have done, something dangerous, and it felt amazing.

But I haven't done anything like that again.

I stood in the courtyard in front of the house with Jas, watching the others drive away.

'I really, really, *really* want to learn to stand on a horse's back,' Jas said.

And I thought of Skye standing on Marigold, the smile on his face, the way he looked like he was flying.

'Me too,' I said.

The Film Diaries of Bluebell Gadsby

Scene Four
The Stream

OUTDOORS. DARTMOOR.

Slow panoramic sweep over the moor.
CAMERAMAN (Blue, off picture) stands
on the wall of the small stone bridge
over the shallow stream which runs
across the moor beyond the paddock
at Horsehill Farm. Heather blooms in
shades of mauve and purple. Gorse
blazes, a fierce yellow. The sun has
turned dry grass to straw, but it is
still lush green where the ground
dips and the water spills into boggy
marshland.

Camera pans east, following the
narrow lane which snakes over the

moor towards the stark rocks of Satan's Tor, 457 metres high and two and a half miles away. Camera lingers for a while, then pans back towards Horsehill Farm, low and white, nestling in its coppice of trees.

JASMINE and TWIG are both in the water upstream from the bridge. Twig wears a snorkel and mask and lies with his face submerged in a rock pool he dammed last summer to create a breeding ground for newts. Jas, in a faded polka-dot bikini which used to belong to Flora, lies on her back in the running water of the stream, her long hair snaking round her body gathering mud and silt.

She is pretending, not very convincingly, to be a water nymph.

CAMERAMAN
(now sitting on wall with feet
dangling over the water)

Did you know that this is an enchanted bridge? Grandpa told me. Apparently,

if you walk along it at full moon
with your own true love, you will be
married within the year.

                    TWIG
            (emerging from the stream)
        I bet that's not even true.

                  JASMINE
        (sits up in the water, hair dripping
              down her back, not remotely
              interested in tales of yore)
    Do you think Skye will *ever* teach me
              to ride without a saddle?

                 CAMERAMAN
              Sure he will.

                  JASMINE
        (not really listening to Cameraman)
        Because I keep asking. And he
                  hasn't yet.

                 CAMERAMAN
        We only *met* him two days ago.

JASMINE
(lower lip starting to wobble)
I want to go home.

CAMERAMAN
What? Jas!

Cameraman is about to stop filming
to comfort Jasmine when Twig (who has
gone back to his rock pool) shouts
out.

TWIG
I've found one! I've found one!
Blue, quick, bring me the jar
and net!

Picture jolts as Cameraman clambers
down from the bridge and paddles
through the water with a large Mason
jar and fishing net, while Twig keeps
his eye fixed on the pool. She hands
him the equipment. He lowers the
net gently to the water, flicks it
over something brown and small and
squirmy, then plunges the jar in the

pool. Bubbles rise to the surface as water replaces air, and he pulls the jar triumphantly out.

Camera zooms in. The newt is about ten centimetres long, brown with dark speckles and a creamy yellow, black-dotted belly. It looks like a cross between a lizard and a frog, and it is paddling round the jar in crazy circles with its little head held out of the water.

TWIG
A female Common Newt! This is so lucky! Normally, they've left the water by now. I didn't think I would find one. I need to get her back to the house and out of the water before she drowns.

He raises the jar to his face and gazes rapturously at his new pet. The newt stops paddling for a second and glares back, before resuming its circular swimming.

CAMERAMAN
She's scared, Twig. I really think
you should put her back.

TWIG
But I want to keep her.

JASMINE
(bringing the conversation back to
her)
And I want to go home! I want to
see Mum and Pumpkin and they're not
here, and now we're like that newt!

TWIG AND CAMERAMAN
(understandably baffled)
Excuse me?

JASMINE
We're trapped, just like her! We
can't get out, and Mum and Pumpkin
will probably never come, just like
Skye will never teach me to ride
bareback or stand on a horse and
it's all Twig's fault.

                    TWIG
                (still baffled)
              What have I done?

                   JASMINE
          YOU DROPPED HIM ON HIS HEAD!

She runs, still dripping, back towards
the house. Twig sighs and tips the jar
into the pool. The newt vanishes with
an indignant swish of its tail.

                  CAMERAMAN
            We'd better go after her.

Camera goes off.

We were all awake this morning when the boys came. Jas set her alarm for half past seven and by the time they arrived she was ready for them, dressed in jodhpurs and boots, with her hair tied back and her riding hat swinging on her arm.

'I asked Grandma and she said yes,' she told Skye. Which was partly true – she did ask Grandma if she could have a riding lesson. She just never mentioned the no saddle part, and Grandma never asked. I think she'd forgotten all about it.

Skye said that was excellent and they should get started at once, just as soon as they did all the other horsey chores. Twig and I had joined them by then, and he said we could all have a go if we wanted. I'm pretty sure he meant it too, because he looked really happy – I think anything involving horses makes Skye happy. But then Ollie said there wasn't time because Lizzie had asked them to paint the spare room for when his parents come, or had he forgotten?

'We've got all day for that,' Skye said.

'And you've got to go to Plumpton for your glasses.'

They stood there staring at each other, and it was like Ollie was trying to say something with his eyes that Skye didn't want to hear, but in the end he shrugged (his shoulder seems much better) and said, 'Tomorrow, Jas, OK?'

It took us a while to gather up all our stuff from the stream – Twig's snorkel and mask and field trip equipment, towels and clothes and shoes and books. The path to the stream gets really overgrown in summer, with nettles and cow parsley and hawthorn. There's not room to walk two together, and we weren't going to catch Jas up after she ran off. I walked slowly with Twig so we could talk.

'Skye *did* say tomorrow,' I insisted. 'I'm sure he'll keep his word.'

'It's not *about* Skye and the stupid horses,' Twig said. 'You heard her. It's all about Pumpkin. It's *always* all about Pumpkin.'

I've never heard Twig sound bitter before. We'd reached the end of the path, where it opens up by the paddock, under the rowan tree near the brambles in front of the barn.

'Let's stop a minute,' I said, and we sat down on the bench, right across the fence from where Hester and Marigold stood dozing in the shade, swishing flies away with their tails.

'I'm sure it's *not* your fault,' I said. 'Mum not coming. I'm sure it's not just because you dropped Pumpkin.'

'It's always about Pumpkin,' Twig repeated. 'And when it's not Pumpkin, it's Jas. It's never about anyone else. It's all how much Jas loves him, and how well she looks after him, and how much she misses him. I know I dropped him, but he was fine and I was trying to help. No one noticed that bit. And I'm reading a massive boring French novel but no one's impressed because *Jas* writes poetry. I made the first eleven at cricket last term, and no one said a thing. No one! Dad loves cricket but he didn't come to a single match. And when Pumpkin was born, in hospital, it was all "I have a son, I have a son". Not "I have *another* son". It's like I don't exist.'

'I'm so sorry . . .'

'It's not *your* fault! It's not even Pumpkin's fault. It's just how it is, I guess. When people have babies.'

I squeezed his hand but I'm not sure it helped.

'What do you want to do?' I asked.

'I don't know, but I can't stay here all summer with just vegetables and ponies. My friend Justin's in Cornwall, which isn't far away at all, but he's learning to surf and stuff. I would love to learn to surf. I don't even *like* ponies. Or vegetables. I used to really like it here, but . . .'

'Everything feels different,' I said.

*

Grandma was in the garden when we came back from the stream, kneeling on one of those foam knee pad things old people like, weeding the dahlia beds.

'Can you tell me what's wrong with your sister?' she asked. 'She came storming past me barefoot in her bikini, left a trail of muddy footprints everywhere then marched back out carrying an exercise book. I asked if she was all right but she said she didn't want to talk.'

'Where did she go?'

Grandma turned and pointed at the old oak tree by the edge of the potager, the one that Iris always used to climb.

'Let's go and talk to her,' I said to Twig, but he said he'd rather not.

'Twig can stay here and talk to me,' Grandma said. 'And explain what on earth is going on.'

I can catch hold of the lower branches of the tree now to swing myself up, but Jas still has to use the old fruit-picking ladder. It was leaning against the trunk, but she'd carried on climbing, right up to the part where Iris liked to sit, the flat bit where four branches meet and if you're small enough you can almost lie down, and she was scribbling away furiously in her poetry book.

'Can I see?'

She hesitated, then handed me the book.

'Read it in your head.'

Jas's poem went like this:

The moor stretches out around us
As far as eye can see
Tors and rocks and sky and water
Ponies roaming free
But I cannot see their beauty
I can't see it at all
The place that once I used to love
Is like a prison now to me

'Oh, Jas,' I said.

I handed back the notebook. She stared down at it.

'I couldn't find a rhyme for water.'

'Is this really how you feel?'

A tear rolled down the end of her nose and splashed onto the page. I put my arm round her. She resisted for a second, and then I felt her stiff little body slump against me.

'What if he forgets me when I'm not there?'

She started to cry properly then, and I hugged her even closer. I tried to imagine what Zoran would say, because he's always good in situations like this, but I couldn't think of anything except, 'He couldn't possibly forget you.'

' He could,' Jas hiccoughed. 'He's only a baby.'

'The hours you spend looking after him. Changing his nappy, cuddling him when he's crying. Playing with him in the bath. Nobody looks after him as well as you do. I bet he remembers everything.'

'Really?' Jas stopped crying.

'What do you miss most about him?' I asked.

Jas looked thoughtful, and I thought maybe it was a stupid question to ask, because it would upset her all over again, but she was smiling.

'The way he blows bubbles and tries to eat his toes.'

'That is very cute,' I agreed.

'And grabs my hair when I cuddle him, and tries to chew my face when I give him butterfly kisses, and curls his toes round my finger when I tickle his feet.'

I tried not to mind that he has never done any of those things with me.

'Do you remember that time when I changed his nappy?' she said. 'And he was all naked and wriggling, and I blew on his tummy and Mum said no don't do that, and I said why not, and then he peed right in my face and she said, that's why?'

I laughed. Jas sighed and looked sad again.

'I miss him so much,' she said.

'I'll tell you what you should do,' I told her. 'You should write him another poem. Not a short one like when he was born. A really, really long one, like an epic or a ballad, telling him everything you're doing here. A sort of record, like I do with my camera. And then when he's older you can read it to him, and I can show him my films, and he'll feel like he was with us all along. What do you think?'

Jas's eyes were shining, but with excitement now, not tears.

'Are you two all right up there?'

We looked down. Grandma and Twig were standing at the foot of the tree.

'We've been talking,' Grandma said. 'And we've had an idea. Come and have some lunch, and then we're driving into Plumpton.'

The trip to Plumpton was to get bicycles. That's what Twig and Grandma talked about while Jas and I were in the tree.

'For exploring,' Twig explained.

'But we have the ponies,' Jas said.

'Only two ponies,' I pointed out. 'And Twig doesn't like them.'

The bikes were hybrids, which means they can go on roads and paths.

'But no riding across the moor,' Grandma said. 'For ecological reasons . . .'

'. . . in case we squash newts or bugs or plants,' Twig explained.

'And for safety.'

'In case we get lost, or stuck in a bog and drown.'

'Drown?' Jas cried.

'People do.'

'The point is,' Grandma said, 'I am trusting you.'

Then we loaded the bikes into the Land Rover and came home. Grandma didn't drive cross-country this time, and we went past Satan's Tor. It was quite late, and the car park at the bottom was almost empty, but there were still a few people at the top.

'I wonder if any of them will stay the night,' Grandma said.

'What, like camp?' Twig asked.

Grandma pulled over on the side of the road, and we all stared up at the tor, which is basically just a massive outcrop of rock at the top of a hill, but which looks very menacing when you are right beneath it.

'You know the story,' Grandma insisted. 'It was one of your grandfather's favourites.'

Jas and Twig shook their heads.

'I don't remember either,' I said.

'About the two lovers? His parents wouldn't allow them to marry because he was rich but she was poor, so they came here together to jump. United in death, they said, except at the last second he didn't do it. And as she jumped she realised he wouldn't follow, so it wasn't the fall that killed her but her own breaking heart.'

'That's horrible,' Jas said.

'And if people come up here alone, they can see the unhappy maiden, still falling,' I said. 'I *do* remember. If you get too close to the edge she'll pull you down with her.'

'People used to come and spend the night up here. Legend had it that if you were brave and pure of heart, you survived and were deemed worthy of love. If not . . .'

'Stop it,' said Jas.

'Your father tried to stay out once,' Grandma said. 'I think he was trying to impress your grandfather. Grandpa always said *he* had done it as a boy. It wasn't true, of course. He never made it past dark, and your father didn't either.'

'Why did Dad want to impress Grandpa?' Twig asked.

'He just wanted attention, I suppose.'

'I would *hate* to sleep out there.'

'Please can we go home?' Jas said. 'I don't want to think about unhappy maidens plunging to their deaths. Plus, I have a poem to write.'

Grandma was tired after the drive and said it was too hot to cook tonight. We made sandwiches for dinner instead and ate them in the garden, in her favourite spot by the potager wall, underneath the climbing roses. It's twilight now, and the air is starting to cool at last. Grandma sent us to fetch lanterns and candles, and they're all around us like a fairy circle. Jas is lying on her front working on her epic poem, with her tongue sticking out the way it does when she concentrates. Twig is lying on his back counting the bats swooping all over the garden. I am writing this and Grandma is just sitting in her deckchair, watching.

'That's at least twenty,' Twig said. 'Where do they come from?'

'The barn, I think,' Grandma said.

'Can I go and look? Do you think there are more?'

Grandma smiled and said why not, but maybe not tonight.

It's almost too dark to write now, even with the candles, but no one wants to go in.

'The hour when witches come out,' Grandma said,

and Jas shunted a bit closer to me and whispered '*Are there witches?*'

'Of course,' I whispered. 'Vampires, too,' and she hit me on the arm.

I'm back in my room now.

A barn owl took off in front of us as we walked back in from the garden. It sailed out of Iris's oak tree like a ghost and soared past us with a soft whoosh of its wings, out onto the moor with the moon glinting on its back. I know that sounds like one of Jas's poems, but it's exactly how it was.

We all stopped still as statues, the four of us, until it had passed.

'That was spectacular,' Twig breathed.

A newt, bats and a barn owl in one day. Pumpkin issues aside, that's all it takes to make my brother happy. I don't think he even noticed how dark the night was all around us.

Jas, still stuck in epic poetry, said the owl was like the phantom of the girl who died on Satan's Tor. Grandma said that every time she sees something like that it makes her love Horsehill a little more, and I saw Jas slip her hand into hers, like she was saying she loved it too.

For me, that owl was like a message from Iris.

And I'm glad I didn't go to Spain.

The boys came on their bikes this morning, with Lizzie following in the car on her way to Plumpton to drop off a tin of brownies she baked last night specially for us. Grandma said thank you, how kind of you, when I could tell what she really wanted to say was 'Really, Lizzie, I am perfectly capable of making brownies for my grandchildren', but Lizzie didn't notice.

'I can't stop,' she said. 'I have to rush off to fill up the fridge. Ollie's parents are coming tomorrow to stay for a few days. We're really looking forward to it, aren't we Ollie?'

Ollie said, 'Yes, we are.'

'I shall make banana bread for tea,' said Grandma.

Jas asked Skye, '*Today* will you teach me to ride without a saddle?'

Skye, who had been squinting at the back of his hand through his new glasses (exactly the same as the last ones but without the sticking plaster), started and said yes, sure, right away.

Twig said, 'We have bikes.'

'Bikes?' Lizzie cried. 'All of you? How wonderful! The boys must take you swimming.'

'Swimming?' I said.

'At their special place! Skye, hurry up with those ponies. I'll rush home and make you all a picnic.'

'I can make a picnic,' Grandma said.

Ollie said, shouldn't he and Skye get on with finishing painting the bedroom for his parents? Skye frowned, and it was like yesterday, when it felt like they were fighting silently in the paddock. Lizzie said nonsense, she could do it herself when she got back from Plumpton.

'And what about Elsie?' Ollie said. 'She can't go that far. Last time Skye had to carry her back, and I had to push the bikes home.'

'Elsie can stay with me,' Grandma said. 'We'll both enjoy that.'

Lizzie beamed. 'So everything is decided.' She shoved the cake tin at me. 'Off you go! Take the brownies!'

You can't resist someone like Lizzie Hanratty when she's made her mind up about something. Grandma only just managed to convince her not to go back to make us lunch, and cut some sandwiches herself. Skye promised Jas her lesson when we got back and the two of them went to check on the ponies. Twig and I packed swimming costumes and towels, and within half an hour of Lizzie deciding we should go, we were off.

*

71

I thought I knew our part of the moor quite well, but I had never been where we went today. We cycled for ages. Ollie and Skye rode ahead, pausing from time to time to let the rest of us catch up. I followed last, in case anything happened to Jas or Twig. After maybe fifteen minutes of riding on the road, we turned onto a path. After what felt like ages of that, we left the bikes behind a stone wall and continued on foot, following a narrow, deep, fast stream. And finally, after lots of stumbling and clambering over rocks and tussocks and hopping from one side of the stream to another, we arrived at the pool where the boys go swimming.

It *is* a good pool. The stream's wider there, with a steep bank on one side where the water runs deep, and a meadow on the other with shallower water and a sort of beach. Higher up the slope, towards Satan's Tor and almost covered in bracken, you can just make out the ruins of old stone cottages, and about twenty metres downstream from the beach there's a bridge covered in grass and moss that looks like it's about to fall down.

'The Bridge of Destiny,' Ollie said in a spooky voice. 'You know the story, right?'

'Story?' Jas looked nervous and asked, did people die and were there witches?

'Both,' said Ollie.

'Then I don't want to hear it.'

'You can't swim at the Bridge of Destiny without knowing the story first.'

'If she doesn't want to hear it,' Skye observed, 'you probably shouldn't tell it.'

'She can cover her ears.'

'I'll tell it then. You'll only make it scarier on purpose.'

'Yes, because I'm an awesome storyteller. Way better than you. I'm telling it.'

'Fine,' Skye grumbled. 'You tell it. Just don't blame me if she gets nightmares.'

Ollie sat down cross-legged on the grass and patted the ground beside him.

'Gather ye round,' he said. 'And hear my tale.'

We sat round Ollie in a semi-circle (all except Skye, who sat on a rock with his back to us), and he began.

'Many centuries ago,' Ollie said, 'there was a village here, full of old-fashioned people who believed in the olden ways of magic. But then new people came who didn't think like them. They thought local tales of pixies and nymphs and giants were just stupid, and they especially hated stories about witches. The new people grew more and more powerful, and to

73

show they were superior to the folk who lived here, they announced that they were going to get rid of the witches for good, by drowning them. So they brought them all to this place. On the other side of the bridge, the water is even deeper than it is here, dark and still, with steep banks covered in brambles and trees with branches so thick you can hardly see the sky. The new people pushed the witches one by one off the bridge, and then they threw stones at them, and poked them with long poles. The witches – who weren't really witches at all, just ordinary women – cried for mercy, and sought refuge under the bridge, but they all drowned. All except one, an old hag called Melisandra, who went last. When her time came, she didn't wait to be pushed, but leaped onto the side of the bridge. She raised her arms above her head and they all stepped back in fear, because Melisandra had begun to glow and she didn't look like a hag any more but a beautiful young woman with waist-length hair the colour of spun gold. 'I curse you!' Melisandra cried. 'I curse you, and your children, and your children's children!' And then, in a blinding flash of light, she leaped. When the men could see again, they all gasped. The water of the pool had turned a bright turquoise blue, the brambles were full of flowers, and sunlight poured through the trees. That's when they realised how foolish they had been.'

Ollie *is* a good storyteller. We all leaned forward, even Jas, waiting for more.

'Then what happened?' Twig asked.

'That night, a fire started in one of the cottages in the village, and no amount of water could put it out. The fire spread and spread until all the houses were burning, and the villagers were forced to leave and never came back. To this day, they say the souls of the innocents who died that day still haunt the bridge, but . . .'

'What?' whispered Jas.

'The only way to reach Melisandra's pool is from the water. They say that whoever is brave enough to swim under the bridge and out into the pool will achieve whatever is their heart's desire. But whoever falls under its shadow and dares not swim right through will be cursed, just like the villagers of old.'

There was a long silence after Ollie finished, in which we all stared at the bridge.

'*Whatever* our heart desires?' Jas asked.

'Absolutely whatever you want,' Ollie replied.

'Then I'm doing it,' Jas declared.

'You are not,' I said. 'I forbid it. It's dark under

there, you're not a strong swimmer, it looks really dangerous.'

'I *am* a good swimmer.' Jas had already stripped off her shorts and T-shirt and was dancing on the edge of the stream in her swimming costume.

'Film me!' she ordered, and she splashed into the shallows.

The Film Diaries of Bluebell Gadsby

Scene Five
The Bridge of Destiny

JASMINE squeals as she throws herself
from the shallows into the deep water.
The current is quite strong, and
carries her fast towards the bridge.
Picture jolts up and down as CAMERAMAN
(BLUEBELL, worried) runs along the
bank to keep up.

                    JASMINE
   (a bit panicky, doing doggy paddle)
   AGGGHH! I'm going to hit the bridge!

                    OLLIE
      (keeps up with her easily doing
                breaststroke)
   Trust me, we do this all the time. It
    slows right down. Just go with it.

OLLIE is right. The current slackens as they approach, but there are only a couple of feet between the water and the bottom of the bridge on which Cameraman now stands, still filming but trying to discourage Jasmine, who is directly beneath her with Ollie, treading water.

OLLIE

The souls of the dead! The witch's curse! Are you sure you're brave enough?

CAMERAMAN

Jas, I am ordering you to turn back.

JAS

Let's go!

Her doggy paddle is frantic now, but she keeps her head above water and stares straight ahead. Ollie follows, and they both disappear from sight.

DISEMBODIED VOICES FROM
BENEATH THE BRIDGE
Whoooooo! Whoooooo! MWAHAHAHAHAHA!!!!

Cameraman crosses bridge and focuses
on Melisandra's pool, which is exactly
as Ollie described it - tall banks,
brambles, still, dark water, not a hint
of turquoise. Eerie silence, until Jas
and Ollie shoot into it.

                    JASMINE
    I did it! I did it! Ollie made me
   stop and count to ten and I thought
    I was going to DIE I was so scared
              but I DID IT!!

She dives under the water and shoots
back up like a little duck. She shakes
her head, laughing.

                 JASMINE (ctd)
          That was the most fun thing
               I ever did!

Skye and Twig were both very quiet when I came back from filming Jas.

'She's not scared then,' I said, to break the silence.

Skye glanced over to the stream, where Jas and Ollie were still swimming back and forth, whooping and calling out so their voices echoed under the bridge.

'It *is* a good story,' I said. 'I'm sure you'd have told it just as well. Better.'

'No, Ollie's right,' he admitted. 'He's much better at stories than I am.'

'I don't know how she does that.' Twig was staring at the dark space under the bridge. Jas had bobbed up on our side for the third time, and was waving, shouting at us to come too.

'It is quite fun,' Skye said. 'There was a branch stuck under the bridge last time, it felt like a hand trying to pull you down.'

Twig shuddered. Then Jas came running back and threw herself down next to him, followed by Ollie.

'You have to do it, Twig!' Jas said. 'It's amazing!'

She whispered something in his ear, but he shook his head.

'It'll work if we both wish it!' Jas urged.

'I don't feel like it.'

'Dude, for your sister!' Ollie said.

'Leave him alone,' I murmured.

Ollie's eyes widened. 'What, is he scared?'

'That pool is creepy,' I said.

'Twig doesn't like the dark,' Jas said.

'Seriously?'

Twig stood up and started to walk away.

'Wait!' Skye jumped up too, tripped over his undone laces as usual, straightened his glasses, grabbed his rucksack and ran after Twig. 'This way!' he yelled. Twig turned round and Skye pointed at the ruined village, waving his arms about like a sort of friendly, demented windmill. 'Let's go and explore!'

Twig shrugged, but changed direction.

'I just thought it would help my wish come true. I wished for . . .'

'Shh!' said Ollie. 'Don't say it out loud, or it won't happen. Blue, you'd better swim under the bridge instead. You're not scared, are you?'

'No!'

And it wasn't fear. Not like Twig, anyway. Not fear of the dark, or witches, or something dragging me down. Just, I know that Jas wished for Mum to come, Pumpkin to be here. And my wish, for the last four years, has always been the same. I know it's hopeless, and I know it won't work, but my wish is always for Iris not to be dead.

You can't wish for a thing like that in public, with lots of people shouting.

'Chicken!'

'Fine!' I got up and walked to the water. 'Are you coming then?'

Jas and Ollie grinned at each other and followed me.

I didn't give them a chance to take cover. As soon as they were close enough, I spun round, hitting the water with the palm of my hand, splashing them. They both squealed (even Ollie), and splashed me back.

I never did make it to the bridge, and no one mentioned it again. Instead, we splashed and swam and dived underwater for ages. Then when we got tired, we lay in the sun and ate our sandwiches and brownies, and then we lay back in the shallows, dozing and talking until Skye and Twig got back.

I wasn't sure about Ollie at first. Maybe because he is *so* good-looking. It's difficult with people like that. You think they're being stand-offish, but actually it's you who's awkward, because you're never quite sure where to look. Ollie wasn't stand-offish at all this afternoon. We talked about loads of things, like how he wants to go to Oxford, and his parents' trip to Italy (Venice, like their honeymoon, and Rome because they love it – Ollie's been loads of times too). And debating, and hockey, and what his favourite films are (*To Kill a Mockingbird* and *Princess Bride*, just like me).

I stayed at the back again on the way home, but this time Ollie went slower so he could cycle with me, while the others went ahead.

'There's an even better place for swimming, if you want to go,' he told me.

'Where?' I asked.

'Secret.'

'Tell me!'

We were nearly home. Ollie stopped cycling and stood leaning against the bars of his bike, laughing at me.

'You'd probably be scared anyway.'

And that's another thing about beautiful people. When they tease you like that, you don't mind. You're just happy to be noticed. They make you feel beautiful too.

'I wouldn't be scared,' I told him.

'Well then,' he said. 'Maybe I'll tell you, maybe I won't.'

He jumped back on his bike and sped off down the hill.

'Wait!' I shouted, and set off after him.

Skye was waiting for us at the turnoff for Horsehill.

'You took your time,' he grumbled.

'Aren't you meant to be giving a riding lesson now?' Ollie asked.

'It's too hot,' Skye said shortly. 'And we have to help Mum.'

Ollie sighed and pushed off on his bike again. 'See you around, Blue!' he shouted without turning round.

Skye *did* turn round to say goodbye. It's not a good idea for anyone not to look where they're going on a bike, but it's an even worse idea for someone like Skye, especially when he tries to wave as well. His bike wobbled and swerved right across the road. He managed to jump off just before it landed in the ditch, but he still stumbled and fell.

Right into a cowpat.

I laughed. I couldn't help myself. It *was* funny.

'Are you OK?' I called.

He didn't answer, and he didn't laugh back. He just picked up his bike and cycled off, but I'm pretty sure he heard me.

And now I feel really bad.

*

The others were in the living room when I got home, with Grandma lying on the sofa, Jas perched on the end talking about her swimming exploits, Twig on the floor trying to get a word in edgeways about the ruined village, and all of them eating banana bread.

'Are you all right?' I asked Grandma.

'She took Elsie for a walk,' Twig said, 'and now she's a bit tired.'

'I'm not tired, I'm hot,' Grandma corrected. 'I had a lovely time with Elsie. I finally taught her to sit. Blue dear, there's a postcard from Zoran on the table in the hall. Go and get it and come and have some tea.'

'I'm just going to take off my swimming things.'

I read the card on my way upstairs.

The picture was of a pretty harbour in Bosnia, with a mosque by the sea. 'It is wonderful to be reunited with family again,' Zoran wrote, and also, 'In a few days we are going to my grandparents' village. I have not been back since I was a boy.'

Zoran used to say *we* were like family to him. I thought back to a few nights ago, when I wished that he was still our nanny. Would things be different if he was here with Mum and Pumpkin? Would we have done everything we did today? I

85

caught sight of myself in the mirror. My face was shiny from suntan lotion and sweat, and my wet hair was completely flat from wearing the cycling helmet, with the two plaits hanging down like drowned rats' tails.

I wasn't beautiful at all.

In my head, this is not what I look like. In my head, I am quiet but a little bit mysterious – mystical, even, like a girl in a story. Everything about me suggests layers and layers of secrets waiting to be discovered. That's what I want people to see, those layers, but it's not what I saw in my reflection this afternoon. What I saw this afternoon was pink and damp and very, very ordinary.

I undid my plaits, plugged in Grandma's ancient hairdryer and dried my hair upside down, not bothering to brush it first. When I looked up again, it was all puffed up in a big fluffy cloud, with my fringe blown to one side.

I stared at it, wondering what to do. Two years ago Flora made her hair into dreadlocks that she dyed pink, and then purple, but I don't think that would work with mine. Then she had it all cut off and dyed it blonde with peroxide, but even she says that was a mistake. In the end I found a piece of black velvet ribbon in the drawer where Grandma keeps her hair pins and used it to tie my hair in a sort of messy bun, with my fringe clipped to the side. It's a sort of Victorian Audrey Hepburn look, like a romantic pixie. I'm not sure it works, but it's a vast improvement on rats' tails.

Saturday 26 July

I woke up late today, and by the time I came down, the kitchen was empty. I poured myself a bowl of cereal and took it out to the garden. Grandma was in the potager, frowning at her bean cage, with Elsie beside her showing off her new sitting skills.

'The others are at the paddock with Skye,' she said.

'Shall I help you here?'

Grandma shook her head. I noticed there were already tiny little beads of sweat at her temples.

'Do you know, I really can't be bothered today. I think I'm just going to sit here in the shade and watch them grow. Your brother's right. Sometimes plants can look after themselves.'

Jas finally got her riding lesson with Skye today. When I joined them she was riding round in a wide circle on Fat Hester's back, without a saddle. Skye and Twig were sitting on the fence, watching her, with Skye calling out instructions while Twig tried to convince him to go with him to the barn in search of bats.

I noticed again how different Skye is when he's around the ponies. He was leaning forward with his elbows on his knees, and I kept expecting him to pitch face first into the paddock, but he didn't even wobble.

'I hate flipping bats,' he said as I walked up.

'But they're amazing!' Twig protested. 'They use radar and echolocation. Tell him, Blue.'

'Bats are amazing,' I said.

Skye shouted at Jas to grip with her knees.

'I'm trying!' Jas bounced past us at a fast trot, waved and fell off.

She lay on her back in the grass, gasping, her chest heaving up and down. It was just like Skye the other day. I jumped down from the fence and started to run towards her, but she sat up, grinning all over her face.

'Get back on then, if you're OK,' Skye said.

Twig announced that he was bored of watching Jas, and that he was going to the barn.

'Good idea,' I said. 'Let's all go.'

Jas said, 'You're only saying that because you're scared I'm going to fall off again,' and Twig said he had to go back to the house to get tools to cut through the brambles to get to the barn.

'You can ride until he gets back,' I told Jas.

She scrambled to her feet, hauled herself back onto Fat Hester and trotted off again, bouncing wildly. I climbed back onto the fence next to Skye. He kept on staring forward, straight at Jas.

'No Ollie today, then,' I said.

Skye mumbled that he'd had gone to the station with Lizzie to meet his mum.

'What about his dad?'

'He's driving down separately,' Skye muttered.

'I'm sorry about yesterday,' I said. 'Laughing, I mean. I truly am.'

Skye shrugged and said he was used to falling off things, and that it didn't even hurt. Jas bounced up to a breathless halt and asked, 'What doesn't hurt?'

'Falling off.'

'It does hurt a bit,' Jas said. 'But it's totally worth it. I'm going to canter now.'

'Here's Twig,' I said. 'Time to stop.'

Twig marched up armed with two sets of garden shears, a scythe, a stick and a rake. Jas glanced at Skye, who shrugged again and said I was right, she needed to learn to trot without bouncing before going any faster. Jas grumbled that we were both boring, but jumped off Hester and undid her bridle.

Twig went first, acting like an explorer, slashing at undergrowth and shouting things like 'After me!' and 'Watch out for snakes!' Even going after someone else, it's hard work cutting through brambles, especially when there are stinging nettles involved as well. By the time we reached the barn we were all sweaty and itchy and a bit shredded, but then Twig pulled a key out of his pocket and turned it in the lock and I forgot about everything and just *wished* I had my camera.

When I was little, Grandpa had a tool bench in the barn where he liked to make things out of wood, shelves and things for the house but also bowls and spoons and little animals. I used to watch him for hours with Flora and Iris, but I think until today no one had been in for years. The sun was behind us as the double doors swung open, and a rectangle of light fell at our feet. There were specks of dust, dancing. Huge cobwebs, heavy with more dust, wafting in the sudden draught. And further in, still in shadows, decades, maybe even centuries of abandoned objects. Grandpa's work bench is still there, covered in tools. There are saws and hammers and chisels, and broken gardening equipment, and ancient agricultural implements which must have belonged to Grandpa's parents and grandparents when Horsehill was still a working farm. We tiptoed round, barely breathing, not daring to touch anything – a trailer for hauling sheep, shears and clippers, an old hand-plough, an actual car (Twig says, a 1940s Morris Minor convertible).

'Cattle stalls,' he observed. They ran down both sides of the barn, stacked with old tyres and jerry cans, their feeding troughs full of milking pails and coils of rope and an old ox's yoke.

'There's a ladder.' Skye pointed to the back of the barn. 'It goes up to a second level. It must be a hayloft or something.'

He put his foot on the bottom rung.

'Be careful!' I said.

'What? I think I can manage a *ladder*.'

'It just doesn't look very safe. There are holes in the floor.'

But Skye was already at the top.

'The floor's fine!' he called down. 'There's a shutter up here, I'm going to open it.'

There was a creak as he pushed the shutter open. Light poured in to the back of the barn. Dust specks swirled again. And then Skye started to shout.

We ran to the bottom of the ladder and peered up.

Bats. We found them. Hundreds of them. Maybe

thousands. Swirling around Skye in a frantic beating of wings, so densely packed you couldn't tell where they started or finished, a black cloud with Skye in the middle of them beating his arms and shouting.

'They're going to suck his blood and kill him!' Jas started to climb up the ladder. I pulled her back down.

'We have to rescue him!' she cried.

'You two go out,' Twig said. 'I'll help Skye. He just needs to keep very calm.'

Skye yelled again. Twig started to climb. Jas began to sob and hid her face in my shoulder. Up above, I could hear Twig tell Skye to stop moving, quiet footsteps to the window, the shutter creaking. Darkness fell again, the dust stopped swirling, and then the boys were coming back down the ladder, with Twig going first, leading the way. When Skye reached the bottom, Twig and I each took one of his arms and guided him to the door. Back outside, he fell to his hands and knees. I thought he was going to be sick, but after a few seconds he stood back up again, and then we all slid to the ground and sat together in a huddle against the warm stone wall.

'I told you I flipping hate bats,' Skye said.

And then we all laughed till our tummies hurt, even Skye eventually, gasping and saying 'Did you see?' and 'That was unbelievable!' Skye told us that when he was only seven, he watched *Dracula* with his dad, and ever since he's been terrified of vampires. Twig said we don't have vampire bats in this country.

'And even if we did, they only really feed on cattle.'

'But weren't *you* scared?' Jas asked.

'Not at all,' Twig said, but he was starting to shake.

'Your teeth are chattering.' Jas threw her arms around him.

'Shock,' I said. 'I think maybe you should have a bath.'

We all got up and started to walk back towards the house. Jas and Twig went ahead. Twig was telling her all about how it felt to be in a bat cloud. Jas was hanging on to his hand and saying how brave he was.

Skye kicked a pebble up the path in front of him as we walked back together, and for a while neither of us said a word.

'You must think I'm even more of an idiot,' he mumbled at last.

'I would have been terrified, if it had been me.'

'Having to be rescued by a little kid.'

He kicked the stone into a bush. Boys are so complicated.

'Twig's not that little,' I said.

'I bet Ollie wouldn't have screamed.'

'Maybe he's never seen *Dracula*.'

And then we walked a few more steps in silence, while I struggled to think what to say to make him feel better.

Skye stopped under the rowan tree to pat the ponies. He pulled Marigold's ears and kissed her nose and then he said, 'You really like him, don't you?'

'Like who?' I asked, but I could feel my cheeks getting hot.

'Ollie.'

'No! I mean, a bit. Sort of. Not like that! He's nice . . .'

I started to pet Hester, hiding my face in her mane.

How do you explain things like that to a boy? Things like, that time I saw you standing on Marigold, it made me feel so alive, like I could do anything too, but Ollie makes me laugh and he is *so* good-looking, which I know is shallow but I can't help it. But you're clumsy and a bit awkward, like me – awkward, I mean, I don't think I'm clumsy – and you're nice to my brother and sister and today you came looking for bats with us even though they scare you, and when you ride you look like you're flying and I would like to take off and soar like that, like you, and I haven't felt like that for ages and ages and ages . . . So I like you too, a lot, just not in the same way.

'Skye! Skye, where are you?'

Lizzie's voice cut in before I got a chance to speak.

'I'd better go,' said Skye.

I sighed and followed him back to the house. Lizzie and Grandma were standing in the courtyard. Ollie sat in the back of the car with a blonde woman wearing very big sunglasses.

'My granddaughter, Bluebell,' Grandma said.

The woman nodded, Lizzie and Skye got into the car, and they all drove away.

'See you tomorrow!' I called after them, but nobody replied.

Jas and Twig are in the bathroom together. Jas found an old bottle of bubble bath in the cupboard and emptied the whole thing in for him. Twig is lying up to his neck in lily-scented foam, and she is sitting on the floor talking to him. The house feels too quiet. I wish Flora was here. Flora would know exactly what to say to Skye. She'd find a way of teasing him, make him laugh at himself but also feel special. And if Iris were here – if Iris were here, she would make *me* feel better. I tried to call Mum at her friend's house, but there was no reply. I left a message asking her to call. When I hung up, Grandma was standing by the front door, watching me.

'Let's go for a walk,' she said.

'What about the others?' I asked as we set out.

'They'll be fine on their own for half an hour,' she said. 'Though why Twig is having a bath in the middle of the day is beyond me.'

I guess nobody told her about the bats.

Sometimes I think Grandma doesn't really need her stick at all. She went striding off across the moor, and I was quite out of breath just trying to keep up with her. We walked to the stream and over the bridge, and then Grandma branched out left, following the line of a tiny tributary (if streams even have tributaries), so narrow the grass almost joined up over it but deep enough to hear water echoing underground. There was a vague track beside it and we picked our way along it, into a dip and out again and back down until the trees around Horsehill disappeared from view.

'Where are we going?' I asked.

Grandma stopped, shaded her eyes and pointed.

'That tree?'

We never walk that way normally. It was like a cartoon picture of a desert oasis. One funny twisted tree standing alone on the moor where the tiny underground stream opened out into a shallow puddle, except instead of the desert there was the moor, with sheep instead of camels, and grass and heather for sand. There was even, on the edge of the puddle, a small pyramid in the shape of a triangular cairn, those stacks of stones that are supposed to show you are on the right path.

Grandma sat down, pulled off her Crocs, slipped her feet into the water and sighed with pleasure. I kicked off my flip-flops and sat beside her.

'We built it.' Grandma nodded at the cairn. 'Your grandfather and me. It started the first time he brought me to Horsehill, when his parents still lived here. We sat here, and he had a stone in his pocket, and he put it in the ground to mark my visit. We did it every visit afterwards, and then whenever anything important happened – our engagement, our wedding. When your father was born, when your parents got married, when your great-grandparents died, when we moved down here after your grandfather retired. When a dog died, when we got new puppies. When each and every one of you was born.'

She didn't actually mention Iris, but we were both thinking of her.

'I kept on adding stones,' Grandma said. 'Stone after stone, as if they could bring her back.'

The water of the puddle swam before my eyes.

'And now the one on top is for William.' She gave a tiny smile. 'I'm sorry, I just can't bring myself to call him Pumpkin.'

I sniffed. Grandma passed me a handkerchief.

'I thought your grandfather was awful when we first met,' she said. 'It was at a party. I was just about to start my first secretarial job. He'd just won some local horse race and was planning to go to America to train race horses. He was a terrible show-off. Then he invited me here for the weekend, I realised I was in love with him, ditched my job and ran away with him to Arizona.'

'Why are you telling me this?'

'People grow on you, Blue. Even babies.'

'Everything's changing,' I said.

'Of course it is. Babies are a big deal. But you mustn't think people don't love you. You mustn't think your mother doesn't love you.'

'Then why isn't she here?'

Grandma took my hand and squeezed it. 'You're not the only one who still misses Iris, Blue.'

She reached into her pocket and pulled out a stone. 'Put it on the stack,' she said.

'Who for?'

'Anyone you want.'

The stone was flat and black, with a seam of silver running through it. I tried to balance it on top of the cairn but it wouldn't stay. I had to move a few other stones around until it found its place. I tried to think of Pumpkin, but I couldn't. Everywhere I go on the moor, there are memories of Iris.

'For Iris then,' I said, and the stone stayed.

It's funny how journeys go faster when you know where you're going. We walked out of the oasis and there was Horsehill, just a few minutes away.

'Why here?' I questioned. 'The cairn, I mean?'

'Why anywhere?' Grandma shrugged. 'We stopped there on a walk. Things are rarely as complicated as we think they are.'

'People are complicated,' I sighed, thinking of Skye again.

'They are,' Grandma agreed. 'But they don't change, fundamentally. Situations change. Circumstances. People, on the whole, remain very much the same.'

The Film Diaries of Bluebell Gadsby (except this time shot by Twig)

Scene Six
A Mysterious Occurrence in a Car Park

Plumpton High Street. A bank, a supermarket, a greengrocer, two charity shops, a tourist information place, an antique shop, a library, a florist, a clothes shop mainly selling anoraks and sunhats, a gift shop mainly selling china pixies.

A baby in a buggy, asleep. A group of German back-packers (wearing anoraks and sunhats). A cocker spaniel doing a poo on the pavement, a passer-by tutting, the spaniel's owner scooping the poop. A woman struggling with shopping bags, trailed by several small children eating ice creams.

Parked cars all the way down the street. A red Vauxhall with a Baby on Board sticker. A blue Honda with a dent in the side. A grey Polo with no distinguishing features whatsoever.

Sound of loud sighing. Picture swings to BLUEBELL and JASMINE, leaning against the wall of the supermarket, also eating ice creams.

> CAMERAMAN (Twig)
> Why are we here again?

> BLUEBELL
> We're helping Grandma shop.

> CAMERAMAN (TWIG)
> (really a bit whingey)
> Except we're not, are we? All we're really doing is waiting around while she chats to her friends.

JASMINE
(licks ice cream drips off her dress)
If I lived in the country, I
wouldn't waste time in shops. I'd get
everything delivered like Mum does,
and spend all my days galloping
about on horseback.

TWIG
(who, ever since the newt and bat
incidents, fancies himself something
of a naturalist)
If I lived in the country, I would
spend my time looking for snakes and
buzzards and rare breeds of frogs.
I'm bored. I'm going back to the car.

Picture goes black, then returns once
Cameraman is in the car park, focused
on a tabby cat napping on the roof of
Grandma's Land Rover (Cameraman at this
point is standing on the back bumper).

CAMERAMAN
(assumes the voice of a wildlife
documentary maker)

Warmed by the tropical sun, the tiger cub sleeps. See how its ears twitch, hear its little snores. Lost in dreams of hunting prey, it is unaware of the approach of predators.

Cameraman hoists himself onto his elbows for a closer look. The Land Rover wobbles. The cat, who is sleeping less deeply than its appearance suggests, springs to its feet, sneers, curves its back, arches it, and bounces to the ground.

CAMERAMAN
(now crouching behind the car,
filming the cat as it trots away)
Observe the grace and agility
which make this creature one of
Nature's most supreme hunters.
But lo! What have we here? Some
humans encroaching on the
tiger's territory ...

Picture swings away from cat as Cameraman zooms in on three people walking towards a parked car. The car is a navy blue BMW. The people are Ollie, his mother (still wearing big sunglasses) and a man in Bermuda shorts and a linen shirt with a large gold watch (presumably his father).

The man and the woman are arguing, though their words can't be heard across the car park. Ollie stands a little apart from them with his hands in his pockets and his head bowed. He looks up as the cat crosses his path, straight at the camera.

He is crying.

Cameraman gasps. Picture jerks. Ollie's expression changes to anger as he wipes the tears from his face.

Camera goes black.

I gave Twig my camera because he was bored. We all went to Plumpton to help Grandma, but I suppose there is only so much grocery shopping a twelve-year-old boy can stand, especially when Grandma has to stop to gossip to almost everybody she meets. He showed me the footage of Ollie and his parents in the Land Rover, while were waiting for Grandma to stop talking to yet another person she knew.

'What happened next?' I asked.

'They drove away.'

'Did you speak to him?'

'He looked so cross.'

'Of course he's cross! You can't go filming people in secret when they don't want to be filmed. There are laws against that and everything. People go to jail for it!'

'I won't go to jail,' Twig said thoughtfully, 'because Ollie won't want people to know I saw him crying.'

I've looked at the film again, a lot. Ollie looks different when he cries. I know that sounds stupid, because everyone does, but it makes him more interesting somehow. Like until now he was just cheerful and handsome and funny, but underneath he's secretly tragic.

Grandma says Lizzie was not looking forward to his parents' visit. She says Ollie's parents are very successful and wealthy, and Lizzie was worried her cottage wasn't up to their usual luxurious standards, and that was why there was so much fussing about getting it ready for them before they arrived.

'How do you know all this?' I asked. 'I thought you didn't like Lizzie.'

'Of course I like Lizzie. She just fusses too much.'

Apart from accidentally filming Ollie in the car park, we didn't see either of the boys today. Lizzie called this morning to say she was taking Skye to the beach again and was it OK if he missed a day with the ponies, while Ollie went out with his parents.

'Why does Skye only ever do things with Lizzie or us?' Twig asked.

Jas said, 'I told you, he hates school, and he doesn't have any friends.'

'I'm sure he does have friends,' I said.

'Some people just aren't made for school,' Grandma said. 'Stop gossiping and go and do something constructive.'

We took the bikes out this afternoon, but it wasn't the same without the boys.

This evening, I experimented with pinning my

plaits around my head like a sort of crown. At first, no one noticed again. The others were all in the living room when I went back downstairs, hunched over one of Grandma's old photo albums.

'It's so cute!' Jas didn't even look up. 'Look, Blue, Grandma and Grandpa on their honeymoon, being young and with a donkey wearing clothes!'

I leaned over the back of the sofa to look. Jas held up the photo album, and there were Grandma and Grandpa, in smart summer clothes looking pretty and handsome, sitting in a cart pulled by a donkey wearing dungarees and a straw hat.

'If I was that donkey, I'd want someone to shoot me,' said Twig.

'All the local donkeys dressed like that,' Grandma told him.

'It doesn't mean they liked it,' Twig replied.

'It is a little bit odd,' I agreed, and then they all looked up and fell about laughing. Jas said I looked like the little Swiss girl in the ancient books up in the attic, the one called Heidi who lived on a mountainside with her grandfather and kept goats.

'She drank their *milk*!' Jas snorted.

'I think you look more like that tennis player off the telly,' Grandma said. 'What's her name – she used to advertise those push-up bras.'

'I don't look like a Swiss goat girl *or* a tennis player,' I protested.

'You don't look like a bra model either,' Grandma said, and the three of them nearly cried they were laughing so much.

'When I was a girl,' Grandma gasped, 'I used to stuff stockings in my bra to make my chest look bigger.'

'Oh, do it, Blue!' Jas cried.

'I am *not* stuffing stockings in my bra!'

'Then I will!' Jas ran out of the room to the scullery, skipped back in with a pair of socks and pounced on me.

'Get off me!' I screeched. 'They're not even clean!'

My hair came undone. The socks ended up somewhere on top of the bookshelf and I think Grandma may have just a tiny bit wet herself.

Monday 28 July

There was a message from Flora on the house answerphone this morning, telling me to Skype her when I woke up.

'What is that on your head?' she demanded.

'It's my Victorian Audrey look,' I said. 'I'm bored with always having plaits.'

'You look like a teacher. No, worse. You look like a librarian.'

'I like librarians.'

'It's the glasses. No, it's the hair. Actually, it's both together.'

'How's the whole film star thing going?' I asked.

There really is nothing Flora likes more than talking about herself. She dropped the subject of my hair like a hot potato, and spent the next five minutes telling me how awesomely wonderful her life is.

'Everyone's so friendly! Oh my God, Brandon *Taylor*!'

'Who?'

Brandon Taylor – Hollywood's biggest heartthrob – is not only the star of Dad's film but he is also, like, HER BEST FRIEND.

'What does Zach think of that?' I asked.

Flora cried that oh my God, she said they were *friends* and why was I reading so much into it, and then she changed the subject and said we had to talk about Gloria's latest post.

'I'm not friends with Gloria,' I told her.

I actually still only have thirteen friends on

Facebook, which is about the number I have in real life and which is perfectly fine with me. Flora, who has one thousand two hundred and ninety three friends, says I am hopeless and how do I ever expect to know anything if I don't talk to people?

Gloria has posted saying she's through with men for ever. 'From now on,' Gloria says, 'it's all about the horses.'

'What does that mean?' I asked.

'I was worried something like this was going to happen.'

'Something like what?'

Flora sighed and said honestly, couldn't I at least *try* and keep up. 'So, you know her dad died just after Zoran and Gloria got together?'

I said obviously I did. I loved Bill. Everybody did.

'Well, Gloria's finally cleared his things out of the flat, and she wants Zoran to move in.'

'The flat over the stables?'

'That's why he went to Bosnia. He's so freaked out by the whole moving in together thing. I was kind of hoping they'd resolved this before he went, but obviously they haven't.'

'They haven't known each other very long,' I said. 'And I don't think there's room for a piano in Gloria's flat. Zoran does need a piano.'

'The point is,' Flora said, 'He has commitment issues.'

I thought about this for a moment. 'What does this have to do with us?' I asked.

'It's Zoran and Gloria!' Flora cried. 'We love them! We want them to be happy!'

'But what can *we* do?'

'Obviously I can't do anything because I'm in New Zealand. So it's up to you lot.'

'We're in *Devon*,' I reminded her. 'Gloria is in London, and Zoran is in Sarajevo.'

'At least you're on the same continent,' Flora said, and then she logged off.

Zoran is one of my thirteen friends. After Flora had gone, I went onto his page. He's posted this photograph of him and his sister, sitting side by side on the edge of a well, and he's written 'Home at last – the well where our grandparents used to come for water'. His sister has her arm round him in the photograph, and he has his head on her shoulder, and the two of them look happy.

I really don't know what Flora thinks I can do, but I sent a friend request to Gloria anyway.

Today is so hot we couldn't move, let alone ride a bike. Skye came and went before any of us were up, even

Jas, and Grandma decided she couldn't be bothered with the garden again and spent the whole afternoon asleep in her deckchair. The ponies are standing in the shade, not even bothering to flick flies away with their tails. The hall with its stone floor is the coolest room in the house. I am sitting on the stairs. Twig is lying on the rug, still ploughing through *Les Misérables*. Jas is on a cushion on the floor, wearing Flora's old bikini and going through more of Grandma's photo albums. Every now and then she shows me a picture she's excited about. The last one was of Grandma and Grandpa, older than in the honeymoon picture but still younger than Mum and Dad are now, standing in front of Horsehill with a dog.

Summer 1968, the caption says. *Horsehill, with Mr Pigeon*.

'No roses,' I remarked. 'They must have planted them later.'

'Look at the dog!' Jas cried. 'She looks just like Elsie!'

I looked closer. 'She really does,' I agreed.

That's the thing about being here. The past and the present are completely mixed up and after a while you stop knowing what's real and what isn't.

New Zealand may be a different continent, but Horsehill is a different world.

The Film Diaries of
Bluebell Gadsby

Scene Seven
The Dinner Party

Evening. The Hanrattys' cottage, inside
and out.

Long shadows, golden evening sun. The
house (much smaller than Horsehill) is
of grey stone, with white painted gables
and a thatched roof. Creeper climbs up
the wall. There is a small conservatory
at the back. The garden is large,
mainly lawn, with a couple of trees and
beds of tall white daisies, pink asters,
mallow and rosemary. At the bottom,
half hidden by rhododendrons, is an
oversized shed, painted duck-egg blue
with teal green trimmings (the fruit
of Skye and Ollie's labours). A string
of lights around the door make it look
like a fairy cottage.

A white metal table stands on the lawn, with matching chairs turned towards the moor, stretched out beyond a tumbledown stone wall. There is a bottle of white wine in a cooler, a jug of lemonade, coloured glass tumblers. GRANDMA and LIZZIE sit at the table. JASMINE sits in the tree above them, boasting about her new bareback riding skills (she does not mention falling off). TWIG and SKYE sit on a rug, also beneath the tree, with ELSIE. Skye is polishing an old bridle, while Twig talks him through the plot of *Les Misérables* (Fantine has just sold all her hair, and also her teeth) and Elsie chews somebody's trainer.

                    TWIG
                (unconvincingly)
    I swear it's better than the film.

It all looks like a photograph from a magazine.

Cameraman wanders indoors, through

the conservatory to a small country kitchen, where cupboards painted the same duck-egg blue as the shed match the patterned Indian cloth thrown over a table groaning with food, including: a large roasted ham, fried chicken, sausages, tuna pasta, potato salad, tomato salad, green beans, crisps, three kinds of cheese, bread rolls, sliced bread, pitta bread, a chocolate cake, homemade shortbread and a large bowl of strawberries with soft whipped cream, a jug of wild flowers and lots and lots of candles.

Lizzie bustles in, claps her hands, then goes to the sideboard, picks up a large brass bell and shakes it vigorously. Cameraman steps aside to avoid being deafened.

People start to drift in from the garden. Lizzie surveys her dinner table, wonders absurdly whether she has made enough food, urges people to pick up plates, help themselves and take their food back out to the garden.

A door opens at the back of the room and OLLIE enters. Blue jeans, clean pressed preppy American T-shirt, freshly tousled hair. He looks as perfect as ever, but his eyes are rimmed with red.

Lizzie frowns at Cameraman.

Camera goes off.

Lizzie came round this morning to invite us to dinner. 'A simple picnic supper,' she said. 'To cheer us all up.'

'Do we need cheering?' Grandma enquired, and Lizzie went a bit pink and said she certainly did, because her visitors had left early and the house felt very empty.

I could see Grandma was trying to think of ways of saying no, but Lizzie insisted. 'It would mean a lot to me,' she said. 'To say thank you, for everything you have done for us.'

'Done for you?'

'Making us so welcome,' Lizzie explained, and Grandma looked a little bit ashamed of herself.

Mum called at last after Lizzie had gone. Jas spoke to her for ages. Pumpkin has cut his first tooth and is crying a lot. Jas got a bit teary then and asked Mum to email photos so she could see it, and also told her to buy gel at the chemist to rub on his gums so they wouldn't hurt so much.

'I read about it on the internet,' she said.

Mum said thank you, and wasn't she lucky to have Jas to remind her of these things, and I think Jas honestly believed Mum would never have thought of it without her, because she beamed and rushed straight off to compose a verse all about teeth. Then Twig told her all about the newt, but not the bats, because we agreed grown-ups probably didn't need to know about that, and then it was my turn to talk to her. I asked her when she was coming, and she said she didn't know.

'This teething business is very exhausting,' she said, and then I wanted to talk to her about Iris and Pumpkin and Ollie and Skye, but I couldn't find the words.

'Can I get contact lenses?' I asked. 'Flora says I look like a librarian.'

'You like librarians.'

'It doesn't mean I want to look like one.'

'All that sterilising and poking things in your eyes,' she said.

'You can get disposable lenses. I googled it.'

'Guess how many bottles I sterilised today?' Mum asked.

The answer was lots. Also brushes, teats, dummies and little plastic spoons. That was pretty much the end of our conversation. Grandma was quite sniffy when I told her, and said in her day babies were encouraged to crawl around in the dirt to boost their immune systems, and nobody ever sterilised a thing.

'Your father once ate a snail,' she told us. 'A live one, I mean. Not with sauce.'

'Is that actually true?' Twig said.

'And can I get contact lenses in Plumpton this afternoon?' I asked.

'You don't need lenses,' Grandma said. 'You're beautiful just the way you are.'

Flora messaged again. I told her about tonight, and she asked what I was going to wear.

'Oh for God's sake,' she said, when I told her I hadn't thought about it.

Flora says you should always look your best for parties, because that's when you can impress the most people at once. Dad took her with him to a film premiere just after Pumpkin was born. Flora always looks amazing but that night, knowing there would be film stars and agents and all sorts in the crowd, she really went for it. She bought new strappy sandals specially, with heels so high she couldn't walk down stairs in them. She wore them with skinny snakeskin jeans, frilly socks, a ripped rock band T-shirt and a man's dinner jacket, with gold glitter on her face, purple lipstick and her short blonde hair spiked up all over her head. She called it her glamorous rock-chick pixie grunge look.

'Do something like that,' she messaged.

'I don't think I can pull off glamorous rock-chick pixie grunge,' I wrote. 'I think it might be a little overwhelming. Plus I think I'm more mysterious and mystical.'

'Tone it down then, but do *something*. Send pictures. If I find out you went out to meet two boys wearing denim cut-offs and a tank top, I'll disown you.'

It's hard to look mysterious and mystical when the only clothes you own are jeans and shorts and flip-flops and your grandmother won't buy you contact lenses. In the end, I found a long strappy minty green silk top in the closet where Grandma keeps the clothes she doesn't wear any more, and I wore that over some white leggings of Jas's (very short on me), with green flip-flops, some pink lip gloss Flora must have left on her last visit and my hair piled up on top of my head with artistic tendrils hanging down to frame my face.

'Goodness,' Grandma said when she saw me. 'My old nightdress.'

'Nice toothpaste,' Jas said.

'Fresh,' Twig agreed, and they both cracked up.

I don't think Skye noticed for a minute what I was wearing, but Ollie did. After Lizzie rang the dinner bell everyone piled their plates with food, then drifted back out again towards the garden. I was going to go too, but he stopped at the top of the conservatory steps and suggested we sit there.

'I like your top,' he said. 'Is it vintage?'

I told him it was Grandma's nightie, and he was quite impressed.

'Wearing nightclothes at parties is cool,' he said.

And then it was a bit awkward because even though he'd been nice about my clothes I knew I was going to have to say something about the car park but I didn't know how.

'Lots of the girls at school like vintage stuff,' Ollie said. 'That's how I know about it. There are loads of shops in Bath. You should come, if you're into it. I could show you.'

'I'm sorry we saw you crying,' I blurted out, and he fell silent and then it was *really* awkward.

'Twig was filming a cat. I've deleted it all. We weren't spying or anything. I just wanted you to know. Also, to apologise.'

'It's fine.' Ollie was a bit red. I focused on cutting up a piece of chicken. A potato shot off my plate. Ollie stared at it. I wondered if I should leave it or pick it up.

'I was upset because they had to leave early.' He

spoke so low I had to lean in really close to hear him. 'They were meant to stay a few days, but they're super-busy. They have these really high-powered jobs, and they've just been to Italy, you know, for their anniversary. They were all, we have to go back early, and I was going to go back with them, then Lizzie said why didn't I stay longer, and I can go to France with them next week.'

'France?'

'To see Skye's dad.'

'Next week?'

'Maybe sooner. I'm not sure. It'll be nice, I guess. I was just upset because I thought they'd be sticking around for longer.'

'It's OK.' I tried not to think about Ollie and Skye going to France. 'Our baby brother . . .' And I told him about Pumpkin, and Mum and Dad being so tired and busy all the time, and Mum not coming and Dad being in New Zealand and no one having time for anyone any more, and then I got a lump in my throat and had to stop. I looked across the garden to where Skye and Twig and Jas were sitting, a little apart from Lizzie and Grandma.

'I knew you'd understand,' Ollie murmured and I blushed a bit.

Night was falling and the bats were out again.

Twig and Jas were sitting back to back with their heads tilted up on each other's shoulders, watching them, with Skye lying beside them on his back.

'They look like they're dancing,' I heard him say. 'I can't believe I used to be scared of them.'

And that made me smile, but then I thought of the owl the other night, how it felt like a message from Iris, and I remembered another time when our parents were too busy, right after she died, when they just worked and travelled non-stop rather than come home and be in a place where she wasn't.

'I had this twin sister called Iris.' I thought it might help, him knowing, but I don't even know if he heard, because he never responded and he was cheerful again, calling out across the garden to Skye, something about tomorrow, and should we go to the river at Tarby. Skye looked round and saw us sitting together.

'Sure,' he said. 'Why not?'

And then Jas and Twig wanted to know all about it, and what time we should leave, and maybe it was a good thing not to talk about Iris. Maybe I still talk about her too much.

Gardens always smell sweeter at night. I'm sitting at my window seat, with the windows wide open, and it smells of roses and grass and chamomile and something else, too, the smell of the moor, which is earth and gorse and animals. I've never seen so many stars, like a little child throwing glitter on a painting, and I can hear the owl out hunting, and Fat Hester and Marigold snuffling in the paddock. The bats are going crazy, feeding on night insects, and Skye's right.

They do look like they're dancing.

The Film Diaries of Bluebell Gadsby

Scene Eight
The River at Tarby

Exterior. The river at Tarby is wide and slow, with a channel of deep green water a few metres long and a couple wide before the banks narrow again. To get to the channel you either have to paddle through the shallows, with your feet sinking into mud, or cross upstream using boulders as stepping stones, coming back to just above the deepest point and swinging out over the water on a rope tied to an overhanging branch.

CAMERAMAN sits on a towel on the grass on the shallow side of the river, filming JASMINE, TWIG and SKYE as they take turns to swing from the rope, competing to see who can make the loudest noise as they land in the water.

Styles differ. Elsie barks her head off throughout proceedings.

JASMINE
(hangs from the rope, hovering above the water, screaming)
It's so high! IT'S SO HIGH! LOOK AT ME!

SKYE
(scrambles a bit too enthusiastically off the bank, swings back, hits the tree, lurches back to the middle of the river, lets go and lands in a perfect belly flop)
AAAAAAAAGGGGGGGGGGGGGGGGGHHHHHH!

OLLIE, sitting on the river bank next to Cameraman, laughs out loud. Cameraman looks at him reproachfully.

OLLIE
What? It was funny.

                    TWIG
              (climbs up the rope)
        It's only a two-foot drop from where
        you were, Jas. I want to go higher.

                   JASMINE
        NO, TWIG, YOU'RE GOING TO DIE!

                    TWIG
           I'm ... really ... really ...
                good at climbing.

Jasmine and Skye tread water,
shouting up encouragements as Twig,
looking a little bit like a monkey
and a little bit like a frog, climbs
the rope all the way to the top and
touches the branch. Cameraman shouts
too. Twig beams, looks down and
gulps.

                   CAMERAMAN
                  (anxious)
        Come back down a bit before you jump.

Twig slithers down carefully, as he has been taught to do in gym classes at school. When he is about three feet above the stream (which is still higher than Jasmine and Skye), he lets go and drops into the water with a surprised squeak. Elsie hurls herself in after him, barking louder than ever.

I wanted to mess about in the water with the others, but Ollie asked if we could go for a walk instead.

'I don't feel like swimming,' he sort of whispered, and I realised he was probably still upset about his parents.

'Seriously?' Skye looked incredulous. 'A walk?'

I tried to roll my eyes at him without anyone noticing, like I was telling him I was just doing it to make Ollie feel better, but I don't think he understood.

'I'll film you all first,' I offered, and he shrugged and said, 'whatever makes you happy.'

'Maybe we should stay,' I said, after the belly flop.

'You'll only embarrass him more,' Ollie said.

Out of sight, beyond the bend in the river hiding them from view, Skye, Twig and Jas had started to sing. I think the game was to get through as much of a show song as possible before hitting the water. Jas sang 'Let It Go' from *Frozen*. Twig sang 'Do You Hear the People Sing' from *Les Misérables*. Skye sang 'Gee Officer Krupke' from *West Side Story*, very loudly. He actually has a really nice voice.

Ollie and I took our shoes off and he dared me to stand still as mud squelched through my toes and my feet completely disappeared, and then I sat on a rock in the middle of the river while he waded into the deeper water, and there were bright blue dragonflies, and tall pink flowers on the bank, and all the time the singing from round the corner got louder and louder.

I started to hum 'Officer Krupke'. Ollie climbed onto the rock next to me.

'This isn't even a proper river,' he said. 'More of a glorified stream. Do you remember, the first time we went out together, all of us, to Melisandra's pool? I said there was another place we could go?'

'You said I'd be scared,' I remembered.

'Wanna go?'

'What, just the two of us?'

'It'll be most of the day.'

Our feet were in the water and the sun was at our back, and just sitting there with Ollie on that rock in the middle of the river felt dangerous. I couldn't imagine a whole day. The singing was getting louder and closer. The others had left the pool and were already walking towards us. Part of me wanted to run to meet them.

Another part of me wanted to stay.

Ollie smiled.

'Sure,' I said.

Elsie came crashing round the corner, followed by Skye and the others, all singing *Les Misérables* now. Skye's eyes fell on Ollie's hand, which was on my back, helping me out of the water.

His face fell. My heart sank. But Ollie kept on smiling.

The Film Diaries of Bluebell Gadsby

Scene Nine
New Bridge

EXTERIOR. DAY.

CAMERAMAN (BLUE) stands on the towpath on the banks of the River Ealme. The view here is very different from the streams of Dartmoor. Camera spans people walking, a scattering of houses, the ribbon of a road with light but steady traffic, an empty crisp packet floating in the water, discarded drinks cans.

The waters of the Ealme are dark and deep, its banks about a dozen metres apart. The Ealme is most definitely a proper river. New Bridge is so big a two-lane road runs across it, with a white line down the middle and a narrow pavement for pedestrians. There are railings along the sides of the bridge, and on the other side of the railings there is a ledge, and on the ledge, waiting in line to jump, stand OLLIE and a gaggle of local boys.

OLLIE
(waving, now at the front of the line) Have you got me?

CAMERAMAN
(shouts)
Yes.

OLLIE
OK, count me in!

Cameraman begins to count. On three, Ollie yells, then jumps, straight as an arrow, arms crossed across his chest. He barely makes a ripple as he enters the water and disappears from view, for so long Cameraman begins to worry.

CAMERAMAN

(panicking)

Ollie? OLLIE WHERE ARE YOU?

Ollie resurfaces in a spray of water, shaking his head and yelling. He waves and starts to swim towards the bank, where he squelches through muddy shallows towards Cameraman. Behind him, the local boys plop one after another into the water, whooping as they go.

OLLIE

Did you get that? Did you get it? Did you get me?

He hops from one foot to another as he rubs his back with a towel, teeth chattering. Cameraman does not respond. Ollie stops hopping and grins a slow wicked grin at the camera. His hair is tousled and sticking up. His blue eyes dance in his lightly golden face.

OLLIE

That was so awesome! You have to do
it! I'll film you!

Cameraman does not respond. Ollie
stops hopping. His familiar smirk
returns.

OLLIE
You're scared.

CAMERAMAN
I am not.

OLLIE
I don't blame you. It's super-high.

CAMERAMAN
I don't think it's that high.

OLLIE
(reaches out for camera)
Prove it! And show me how this works.

Picture goes upside down and every
which way as Cameraman (Bluebell)

teaches Ollie how to use camera, then settles and focuses on Bluebell as she trudges up the path to the bridge where the local boys have gathered again. They cheer as she drags her feet towards them, and make way for her to climb over the railings.

She doesn't want to go, but it is like someone (Ollie) has cast a spell on her, and she has no choice but to do as he says.

Bluebell stands with her back to the solid bridge, facing the void. You can't see it on camera, but her knees are shaking. Everything is blurred (partly from fear, partly because she is not wearing her glasses). She feels sick and is trying very hard not to cry.

CAMERAMAN (OLLIE)
You can't chicken out now!

Bluebell squeaks. Behind her, the local boys start to shuffle, impatient for their turn. One of them mutters

'Get on with it'. Another tells him to shut it, then informs Blue they haven't got all day.

LOCAL BOY
Just close your eyes and jump.

CAMERAMAN (Ollie) starts to make clucking noises.

And Bluebell does exactly as she is told. She closes her eyes and jumps. Limbs flailing, she screams all the way down, hits the water with a painful smack and vanishes under the surface. Camera focuses on empty water. A few seconds later, Bluebell's head bobs up. She gasps and splutters and laughs and cries as she swims in an unsteady crawl to the river bank.

BLUEBELL
(teeth chattering, wrapped
in a towel)
Did you get me? Can I see? I want
to do it again!

Ollie woke me up this morning by throwing pebbles through my window.

'Hurry up!' he called up when I looked out. 'Skye's still having breakfast. I want to go before he gets here.'

Grandma was already in the kitchen when I went down, drinking tea.

'Too hot to sleep,' she said. 'Someone's up early.'

'Ollie wants me to go on a bike ride with him. It'll be all day. Can I?'

'Where?'

'He's just outside in the garden. I'll ask him.'

Ollie came in and told Grandma we were going to cycle past Abbotsford and hike to a stone circle. 'I read all about it in a book,' he said. 'It sounds really interesting.'

Grandma believed him. I bolted a bowl of cereal. Ollie gobbled one down too. Grandma made sandwiches and walked us as far as the gate.

'Wear your helmet.' She hugged me. 'Take your phone. Stop growing up so fast.'

We were late coming home. It took us nearly two hours to get to the bridge, and even longer coming back. Every bone in my body aches from so much cycling, but it was worth it. Not just the jumping, the whole day. Flying down the last hill coming home, we took our feet off the pedals and stuck our legs out in front of us, going so fast my eyes were streaming by the time we got to the turning to Horsehill, and I felt . . . alive.

I jumped off a bridge. I *never* do things like that.

It was amazing.

Ollie stopped at the corner with me, and his eyes were sparkling as much as mine.

'Shall we do something again tomorrow?' he asked, and I said 'Yes!' because that feeling, flying through the air, disappearing under water – it's terrifying, but I want to do it again.

Putting my bike away and going into the house, I felt like a completely different person, but they barely seemed to notice I was back. Jas was sitting at the kitchen table when I went in, painting. Grandma and Twig were baking a cake.

'To use up all the eggs Lizzie keeps bringing,' Jas said without looking up. 'I'm doing a picture for Pumpkin, to go with my poem. It's us at the stream.'

'Are those our ponies?' I asked. Jas's paintings are always a bit approximate.

'We took them, to cool them down. Skye said we

should. We rode them bareback through the water, a really long way, even Twig.'

'Why *even Twig*?' Twig asked.

'And four people,' I said.

I wanted to jump up and down and shout, 'look at me!' I wanted them to realise how changed I was, but still they just carried on as normal.

'The people are me, Twig, Skye and Grandma,' Jas said. 'We had a picnic. Grandma says tomorrow she's going to wear her bikini.'

'Her bikini!'

'And why not?' Grandma held a floury cheek out to be kissed. 'Did you have a nice day?'

'I don't like Ollie any more.' Jas frowned at her painting, and started adding splodges of bright violet all over the landscape, which I think were meant to be heather. 'He laughs at Skye, and lied to me, and he only ever pays attention to Blue.'

'Be nice, Jas,' Grandma said.

'Did you know they were going to France?' Twig asked.

'Ollie did mention it.'

'They're going on Sunday.'

'On Sunday!'

'To see Skye's dad.' Jas began to flick yellow paint over her picture. 'Gorse,' she explained. 'And he does lie. He said my wish would come true if I swam in Melisandra's pool, but it hasn't.'

'It might still,' I said. She rolled her eyes, and carried on flicking.

Zoran has decided to stay longer in Bosnia. Flora says it was all over Gloria's Facebook. For someone with a busy film career, she has an awful lot of time on her hands.

'They quarrelled,' Flora said. 'She was angry because he said he didn't know when he would come back. He said he felt he was finally putting down roots in the land of his birth and she should give him time.

'Zoran said that on Facebook?'

'I think he thought he was sending a private message,' Flora said. 'Have you got a plan yet?'

'No,' I said. 'But I think you should probably leave them to sort out their problems on their own.'

'I suppose now you're in love with the cousin you think you're some sort of relationship expert.'

'What? I'm not in love with anyone! What do you mean?'

'Talking to him all night ... Cycling off on your own ... What did you *do* all day?'

'It's none of your business! *How do you know*?'

'Jas told me.'

'At least I'm not cheating on my boyfriend with a film star!'

Flora posted a yawning emoticon.

'You're a fine one to lecture me on constancy,' she wrote. 'For a while, I thought you liked the other one. The acrobat with the death wish.'

'You're the most annoying sister ever!' I told her.

Flora wrote HAHAHAHAHAHAHAHAHA and logged off.

Friday 1 August

I'm beginning to understand why Grandma feels the way she does about Lizzie Hanratty.

And I am furious with Ollie and Skye.

Yesterday, when we said goodbye, Ollie said we shouldn't tell anyone where we'd been. He said it should be a secret, because grown-ups can be funny about things like jumping off bridges.

'They overreact,' he said. 'Especially Auntie Lizzie.'

So I lied. When Grandma and Jas and Twig eventually got round to asking what we had done, I DID NOT SQUEAK.

'A picnic,' I said. 'A long bike ride. That stone circle thing.'

'Is that *all*?' Jas said, but Grandma told her to stop pestering me, and that I was entitled to a bit of privacy.

I love Grandma when she's like that.

Then this afternoon Lizzie Hanratty drove up, looking all serious with a fruitcake and yet more eggs, and basically told Grandma everything, because OLLIE TOLD SKYE WHAT WE'D DONE.

AND SKYE TOLD LIZZIE.

Lizzie is not the only grown-up who overreacts.

Grandma hasn't yelled at me so much since Iris and I ate a load of Christmas lunch trifle on Christmas Eve when we were five.

'You lied to me!' she shouted. 'A boy was badly injured last year jumping off that bridge. You of all people, Blue! How could you be so irresponsible!'

'I don't know,' I said, but apparently I am now grounded until the end of my life.

'What does that even mean here?' I protested. 'Where am I actually not allowed to go?'

'ANYWHERE!' Grandma roared.

'WELL I DIDN'T WANT TO COME HERE ANYWAY!' I yelled back.

I felt bad for saying that – really bad. Then I told myself she *was* being unfair.

'Then you'd better pack your bags and leave,' Grandma snapped.

She walked out of the kitchen. I ran out to the garden, and now I am sitting in the oak tree. Twig and Jas were here too, upset because it turns out that neither of them wants to go home any more.

'Skye says I can canter soon,' Jas said.

'Everything's much better than it was,' Twig said.

'Except for Ollie,' Jas reminded him. 'We don't like Ollie any more. Not now that he lies. Especially if he tries to kill Blue. Also, you shouldn't speak to Grandma like that. She's upset.'

'*I'm* upset!' I protested. 'And Ollie did *not* try to kill me!'

And then Skye arrived and stood at the bottom of the tree and said, please could he talk to me?

His glasses were covered in sticking plaster again.

'In private,' he added, when Twig and Jas didn't move.

I tried to ignore him, but it's not easy when you're stuck up a tree and the person you want to get away from is climbing up it. He pulled himself up to a branch just below mine.

'I came to say sorry. For getting you in trouble.'

And then he just sat there pulling bits of bark off the tree, frowning and not saying anything.

'What happened to your glasses?' I asked.

'I had a fight with Ollie.' He rubbed his nose so his glasses ended up crooked, but I don't think he realised. 'He was so pleased with himself.'

'Pleased with himself?'

'All, *guess what I did today* and *dude she likes me way better than you*.'

I blushed.

'So you *hit* him?'

'Only a bit,' he said. 'Then Mum got involved. I wouldn't have told her otherwise. I'm not a sneak. But the kid who hurt himself last year, he went to my school, and she knew all about it so she started to freak out.'

'I can't believe you hit him.'

'Yeah, well, like I said.' He hesitated. 'Ollie's not always cool. He's kind of . . .'

'What?'

'Kind of jealous of me.'

'*Ollie's* jealous of *you*?'

Skye bit his lip. 'I'm sorry,' I said. 'That came out wrong.'

'It doesn't matter.'

I thought he was going to climb down, but he changed his mind and turned back.

'Look, we're going away on Monday. Before we go,

there's this place ... You don't have to come if you don't want to, but ...'

'I'm grounded,' I said, and he said 'Oh', and then he stared up at the leaves, thinking.

'We'd have to go early,' he said. He turned to look at me. 'Like, stupid early.'

'I'll get into trouble again!'

'You won't, I swear you won't. I'll get you back way before anyone knows you're gone.'

'Skye ...'

'I'll wait for you by the kitchen door at five o'clock.'

And then he sort of fell out of the tree and left.

I went back in and messaged Flora and told her everything – Ollie, what we did yesterday, the bridge, Skye.

'They're fighting over you,' Flora messaged back. 'Skye's trying to get back at Ollie.'

'But I don't want that!'

'Oh for goodness sake. Enjoy it. Be crazy!'

'I've been crazy. Look where it got me.'

'Grounded? Pah! Be more crazy.'

Grandma was sitting at the kitchen table with Jas when I came out of the study, shelling peas. Twig told me that Grandma spent the whole afternoon in the potager. 'She didn't even have tea,' he said. 'Or a nap.' She looked up when I came in, but neither of us said anything. I sat down with them, took a handful of peas, and started shelling too. She pushed another handful at me when I'd finished. I looked up, and she gave me the tiniest smile.

'I'm sorry,' I said.

'Never, ever lie to me again,' she said.

Whatever it is we're doing tomorrow, I really hope Grandma never finds out.

Saturday 2 August

Skye was waiting in the shadows outside the kitchen door, just after five o'clock, like he said he would be.

'Where are we going?' My voice sounded really loud in the night. Skye put a finger to his lips and gestured for me to follow him. It was so dark I could only just make out his outline as I followed him towards the paddock. I kept expecting him to trip or something, but he didn't.

Hester and Marigold were waiting, fully tacked up and tethered to the fence.

'We're going riding?'

'You do know how, don't you?' he asked anxiously.

'Of course!'

Riding has actually never been my favourite thing, mainly because most of the riding lessons in my life have consisted either of Grandma yelling at me to GO FASTER, or of Gloria making me fall off. But this morning, following Skye in the dark out of Horsehill and onto the moor, it felt like one of the most exciting things I have ever done.

Riding out in the cold dark just before dawn when you're grounded makes you feel like smugglers coming inland from the sea. Or like highwaymen, back from a night robbing people in carriages, or soldiers setting off for war, or spies out on a mission.

It makes you feel like characters in a book, or from a different country.

Skye kicked Marigold into a trot. Their outline in front of me was solid now, clear black against the sky. I made Hester go faster to catch up with Skye, except that gave Marigold ideas too, and both ponies broke into a canter, but that was fine. I like cantering much better than trotting. Trotting is all jolty. Cantering feels like flying.

So we cantered for a while, not talking, with Elsie running beside us, and I couldn't help this great big smile spreading over my face because it felt so lovely and so magic, and then suddenly Skye was saying 'Whoa there' and we were walking again, and turning off the lane onto Satan's Tor, and I said, 'Seriously?' and Skye said 'Why not?'

Satan's Tor during the day is menacing enough. Satan's Tor when it's not night any more but not yet morning either is a dark mass of land going up, up, up in front of you, and the top all jagged against the skyline looks evil.

'Just stories,' I said.

We swung round and started to climb. The path up was wide and grassy at first, but it ended before we got to the top. There was a sort of low wooden barrier where it stopped that we tied the ponies to, and then we continued on foot up a tiny sheep track twisting through heather and speckled boulders until even that disappeared and we were just climbing the rocks themselves, all the way to the top, when suddenly the whole world dropped away, so steeply and so far I felt dizzy.

The sky was paler now, but the sun hadn't appeared yet.

'No shadows,' I said. 'It's like we're not here at all.'

There's a little hollow up at the top of Satan's Tor, full of the moor's springy, slightly spiky grass, with a smooth rock to lean back on. Skye sat down and started to rummage through his rucksack. I stayed standing, and reached out to touch the rock.

'What are you doing?'

I explained about Grandpa and Dad coming out here to try and spend the night.

'Maybe they sat in this very place,' I said. 'It feels like I could touch them. Like there's a veil or something, and they're just behind it. Like time doesn't really exist. Is that weird?'

'The moor does that to you,' Skye said. 'Do you want a cupcake? Mum made them last night.'

The cake was in a spotted blue case, with swirls of squashed pink icing and a shower of silver balls. I burst out laughing. Skye grinned.

'I know, they're ridiculous. They're all I could find.'

The cupcakes were perfect, just the right balance between light and buttery and sweet. We ate them in silence, licking icing off our fingers while Elsie watched hopefully for crumbs, and all around us the sky got lighter and lighter and faint shadows started to appear.

'When will the sun come?' I asked.

'Soon.'

'There are clouds.' I pointed to a narrow band streaked across the sky.

'Clouds are good. You'll see. Why did your grandpa and your dad want to spend the night here?'

I told him the rest of the story.

'That's even worse than Melisandra,' he said.

'Grandpa told us loads of stories. I can't remember them all because he died when we were quite little, but we used to be terrified of them. Grandma used to shout at him for telling them to us. Then Flora would act them out when we went to bed, and Iris and I would start screaming all over again.'

And then there was a pause, and I wondered if I should explain.

'Iris was my twin,' I said. 'She died.'

'I know. Mum told us, before you came. I'm really sorry.'

And then we sat there in silence for a while, watching the sky get lighter, but it didn't matter that we didn't talk, because somehow being silent was enough.

'Grandpa told us nice stories too,' I said at last, and I told him about the bridge at Horsehill, and being married within the year if you walked on it with your own true love, and Skye said that sounded even creepier than the other stories, and we both laughed. The sound of it woke Elsie. She raised her head with her ears pricked, looking from Skye to me and back again. I patted her head. She sighed and closed her eyes, resting her head on my knee.

'That means you're her friend,' Skye said.

And then . . . I can't even begin to describe the sunrise. Every time I closed my eyes, it was like it was burning inside my eyelids. Every time I opened them, it was a little bit bigger, a sliver and then a giant ball until suddenly it was just there, like it had never gone away. And Skye's right, the clouds were good. It didn't last long, but there was this moment, a few minutes, when the sun was beneath the clouds and they looked like they were on fire, except the fire was bright pink as well as orange and gold, and even the purple sky around them was blazing.

It was like the whole world was being reborn.

Elsie leapt suddenly to her feet, ears pitched forward. Down below, one of the ponies started to neigh. Elsie barked. Skye put his hand on her collar.

'What is it?' I asked.

He pointed. Far beneath us, a herd of wild ponies were galloping towards the tor. Stocky and dark, with tangled manes and tails sweeping the ground and their hooves pounding the ground like drums as they drew closer.

Marigold and Hester started to scream.

'What's wrong with them?'

'They want to join the herd,' Skye said.

He stood right at the edge of the tor, gazing down as the ponies passed. The drum of their hooves grew louder, then fainter as they moved on, disappearing from sight until all that was left was their memory, like a disturbance in the air, and I knew that Skye would give anything to be out there with them too.

Grandma's right when she says Skye's not made for school. He was made for this – wild horses and ancient tors and being outside and free.

The sun rose higher, and the clouds were just clouds again, wisps of grey dissolving in the morning light, and there was the countryside all around us, but somehow it was different from the countryside yesterday. The riding out in the dark, the sunrise. I've never seen Dartmoor like it was this morning – magical and dangerous and new.

Skye let out a long sigh, like he'd been holding his breath, and said we'd best get back to Marigold and Hester. They were still quivering when we reached them, straining at their ropes. Skye whispered to them, pulling their ears, patting their necks. Somewhere out of sight, the wild ponies neighed. We all turned to listen. Hester and Marigold's ears pricked. Elsie raised a paw, ready to run, but the sound was growing fainter and now it was fully daylight. Marigold whinnied. Hester shook herself. Elsie started nosing around after rabbits, and we climbed back in the saddle. The ponies seemed exhausted as we turned towards Horsehill, but their pace picked up closer to home, and we had to slow them down so their hooves wouldn't make too much noise on the road.

We untacked quickly, remembering I was still grounded. It was later than I thought, and Grandma would be getting up soon. We brushed down both the ponies, then let them loose in the paddock.

'Well,' said Skye, and 'Well', I replied.

'Did you like it?' he asked.

'It was amazing,' I said.

'Better than jumping off a lame old bridge, right?' he grinned.

And the thing is, in a way, it was. Jumping off that bridge was so much fun, but when it was over I was a little bit relieved. Whereas this morning . . . I could do that every day of my life and not get tired of it.

But the way Skye was looking at me – it was like now he thought he'd won.

'I had fun with Ollie,' I said.

I took my saddle and bridle to the ponies' shed. I

didn't mean for it to be the last thing we said to each other, but by the time I came out Skye had already gone, and I didn't see him again all day.

And tomorrow they're going to France.

Sunday 3 August

They all came this morning, Lizzie, Skye and Ollie, in the red and white car. I was in my room, and at first I just thought I would stay there, because I couldn't face seeing Skye after the way yesterday ended, or Ollie after all the fuss. But then Jas came and knocked on my door and said that I had to come down, because they were going to France and had come to say goodbye and also that Skye wanted to talk to me.

'What about?'

'*I* don't know, do I?'

I went out through the kitchen. Lizzie was in the potager, talking to Grandma, who was leaning on her shovel, fanning her face with her big gardening hat. I tried to backtrack, but she'd already seen me.

'Ah, Blue!' she cried. 'Don't run away! You mustn't think I'm angry with you, dear. It's my nephew I'm cross with – what was he thinking of, making you

155

jump from that bridge? You must understand I couldn't hide your actions from Granny.'

Grandma rolled her eyes at me.

'I'm sorry,' I mumbled.

'Good girl for apologising,' Grandma said. She looked tired.

'The boys are down at the paddock,' Lizzie said. 'Mind, no antics now! I don't want any broken limbs before we set out!'

I think it was her idea of a joke.

Ollie wasn't at the paddock at all, but hanging around by the car.

'Hey,' he said when he saw me.

'Hey,' I replied.

'Look, I'm sorry about Lizzie and everything. She likes to come over all cool and stuff, but she's kind of extreme sometimes, the way she reacts.'

'You shouldn't have told her.'

'Skye told her!'

'Well, you shouldn't have told Skye. I didn't tell a single person where we'd been. And also . . .'

'Also what?'

'It was dangerous!'

'Ah, come on Blue! Don't be boring.'

'I'm not boring,' I said quietly.

I could see the others at the paddock, the three of

them together, Jas receiving instructions in pony care from Skye, Twig trying to prise a stick out of Elsie's mouth to teach her to fetch, Elsie refusing to drop it. I didn't know then what Skye wanted to say to me, but I knew what I wanted to say to him.

What I didn't say yesterday. About seeing the world being born.

But I never made it to the paddock. I was only halfway down the path when I heard Lizzie call me back. I turned and she was standing on the front doorstep, shouting and beckoning with her arms.

'Your granny's had a turn,' she said when I ran up, and ushered me into the lounge.

Grandma was sitting on the sofa in the living room with her legs up.

'It's nothing to worry about,' Lizzie said, 'but I need to explain what's going on.'

'THERE IS NOTHING GOING ON!' Grandma said, except she couldn't actually shout. She just looked so cross I knew she wanted to.

'What do you mean, a turn?' I asked.

'Foolishness!'

'She fainted,' Lizzie told me.

'For a matter of seconds . . .'

'And bumped her head. I've called the doctor, but he can't come till tomorrow.'

'I could die in the night for all he cares,' Grandma grumbled.

'Grandma's going to die?' Jas appeared in the doorway, looking horrified.

'I thought you said it was nothing?' I said.

'It's nothing,' Grandma sighed.

'You must make sure your granny rests until the doctor comes. She mustn't do anything naughty.'

Twig and Jas giggled. Grandma closed her eyes, but not like someone resting. More like a child hoping everything would go away when she opened them again. I tried to look like the sort of person who can stop her grandmother from doing exactly what she wants. Lizzie asked me to go with her into the kitchen. Skye came too.

'Soup!' Lizzie said, and started hurling vegetables into a pot. 'Watch!'

Skye touched my elbow. 'I need to talk to you,' he whispered.

'If it's about yesterday . . .'

'Just come really quietly.'

'Carrots, celery, onions, garlic!' We tiptoed into the scullery. Lizzie didn't even notice we'd gone. 'I've put Elsie's basket in here,' he said, still whispering, as we tiptoed into the scullery. 'And all her food. She won't be any trouble.'

'You want me to look after her?'

'She really likes you.'

'I really like her too,' I said.

'We can't take her to France. Mum wanted to leave her in kennels, but I know she'd be way happier here.'

Then there was a bit of an awkward moment, like we were both trying to decide if we ought to apologise or not for the way things ended yesterday, and I think we both decided *not*. Skye started to explain what Elsie needed to eat and when, and where she should sleep, and how to call her when she sometimes gets distracted and then Lizzie realised I wasn't paying attention to soup making, saw Elsie's bed in the scullery and said, 'That dog is *not* staying here when the old lady is ill.'

Grandma appeared in the kitchen leaning on her stick. 'Who are you calling an old lady?' Lizzie apologised, and explained about leaving Elsie. Grandma said we would be honoured to look after her, and now please could everybody leave.

'I've called your father,' Lizzie told me before they drove away. 'He isn't answering, of course, because it's the middle of the night in New Zealand, but I've left a message.'

Grandma grumbled that Dad, being on the other side of the world, was even less help than the doctor.

Lizzie said, 'Maybe so, but after that tumble last spring he specifically asked me to keep an eye on you.'

'Like a dog!' Grandma sniffed, but Lizzie ignored her.

Ollie stopped beside me before getting into the car. 'I really am sorry,' he whispered. He kissed me quickly on the cheek. 'Friends?'

I blushed. Skye came out of the house with Twig and Jas, but I don't think he saw.

'I locked Elsie in the scullery,' he said. 'It was your Grandma's idea. She said it was better if she didn't see me go.'

'Good idea,' I said.

'Thanks for looking after her and everything.'

'No problem,' I said. I thought he was going to kiss me too but he did his little wave instead.

After the others had gone, Twig and Jas took Elsie out to play. I sat on the grass next to Grandma in her deckchair.

'Is it because of Friday?' I asked.

'What happened Friday?'

'After our fight Twig said you didn't rest.'

'That!' Grandma cried. 'Of course it's not because of that! I just had a funny turn, that's all. The heat. Sometimes I get dizzy.'

'Zach's grandfather had a funny turn last year,' I said. 'He was in hospital for ages. And Gloria's dad died after a funny turn.'

'Well I am absolutely not going to die,' Grandma said. 'The very idea!'

All the water in Lizzie's soup cooked away while we were out watching Elsie and talking, leaving the vegetables just a burned mess at the bottom of the pan. Grandma said we should have soup out of a tin, and also to make ham sandwiches. She said tinned soup and ham sandwiches are the favourite meal she saves as a treat for emergencies.

'We'll eat in front of the television,' she announced. 'Seeing as I am ill. Blue, look in the freezer and see if there is any ice cream.'

'Are you really ill?' Jas asked.

'Of course not,' Grandma said. 'Let's just pretend.'

There was ice cream, and the rest of Lizzie's chocolate brownies to go with it, with emergency brandy for Grandma and a carton of tropical fruit juice for us, *The Princess Bride* on DVD, with Elsie stretched out on the sofa, twitching happily in her sleep. I took a picture of it all on my camera and posted it on Facebook.

'Finally got a dog!' I wrote, and also 'Love it when Grandma's ill.'

The Film Diaries of Bluebell Gadsby (this time shot by Jasmine)

Scene Ten
The Hound of the Baskervilles

EXTERIOR. DAY.

The stream at Horsehill Farm. The weather is still hot. The sky is bright, bright blue. The air shimmers. The stream is lower than it was at the beginning of the holidays, but it still gurgles and it is still wet. In the water, BLUEBELL and TWIG are fighting a losing battle with ELSIE.

GRANDMA rests in a deckchair beneath a pink tasselled parasol. She wears a long white shirt over a flowered swimsuit, her straw hat, enormous sunglasses and her purple Crocs. On the rock beside her stand a flask of tea and a tin of emergency shortbread. A book lies in her lap, but she is ignoring it, preferring to issue orders instead.

GRANDMA

Talk firmly! Put your hand on her bottom! Push her into the stream!

Skye's trusted, loyal companion has vanished, replaced by Elsie the Evil. The new Elsie twists, she wriggles, she yaps, she growls. She also stinks of fox poo.

NOTE: Rolling in fox poo is one of the things dogs like to do best. To humans, fox poo smells like all the most revolting things you ever smelled rolled into one and left to fester for days in a plastic bag in the sun. To dogs, it's like freshly baked cookies.

Bluebell and Twig want to wash Elsie. Elsie does not want to be washed.

JASMINE

I think you should hug her.

BLUEBELL

(gritting her teeth)

You try hugging her.

GRANDMA

Show her who's boss! Twig, straddle
her! Blue, catch her by the collar!
Get that confounded smell off her!

Confusion, in which Blue and Twig both
try to straddle Elsie. Elsie, sensing
opportunity, twists in her grip and
makes a dash for freedom. Twig lurches
after her, misses, and lands belly
first in the stream, colliding with
Bluebell as he goes. Bluebell's legs
give way under her. She lands on her
bottom in half a foot of water, her
mouth a perfect O of surprise. Elsie,
now believing that the humans want to
play, barrels over, tongue lolling,
and leaps, barking, from one to the
other, jumping over them, licking

their faces, and rubbing as much fox poo on them as she can.

GRANDMA
Oh, my sides! My sides hurt from laughing so much!

Picture wobbles as Jas also doubles up with laughter. Both Bluebell and Twig are fully dressed, but they couldn't be wetter if they were stark naked in the bathtub.

Dad called this morning. Cross, because Flora had shown him my Facebook page, and he thinks we now have a dog.

'Not completely,' I told him. 'I mean, not forever. We're just looking after it.'

'First I get a message from Lizzie Hanratty saying your grandmother is at death's door, then your sister shows me pictures of dogs and all of you carousing.'

'Carousing?'

'Ice cream! Brandy, cakes, and dogs lying on sofas!'

Then Grandma arrived and told me to give her the phone.

'You're fussing again,' she told Dad. 'There is absolutely nothing wrong with me.'

Dad was starting to get annoyed. I could hear bits of what he said even though I didn't have the phone, 'Lizzie said . . .' and 'A dog? A *dog*?'

'I have had dogs before,' Grandma said, and then 'You really must stop worrying about me.'

I went into the kitchen, which was full of smoke from Jas and Twig cooking breakfast.

'Grandma said we should get whatever we wanted,' Twig said. 'Jas wanted sausages.'

I opened the garden door. Elsie bounced in, carrying a stick.

'She kept bashing our legs with it,' Jas said. 'So we put her outside.'

'Drop,' I ordered. Elsie ignored me.

'Well your father shan't bother us again for a while.' Grandma bustled into the kitchen, if you can bustle with a walking stick. 'He's going whale-watching.'

'Whale-watching!' said Twig.

Is this part of your job? I asked him. *No,* he said, *it's part of a well-earned break. Good for you,* I said. *I hope it will make you less stressed.*

Twig said, 'I've *always* wanted to see whales.'

Grandma said, 'Well, my darling, you should have gone to New Zealand with your father,' and then the frying pan caught fire, Elsie began to bark, and the doctor arrived.

Looking through his eyes, I suppose we weren't very impressive. Grandma before she gets dressed looks *mad*, with grey hair down to her waist, her old floor-length nightdress, Grandpa's dressing gown and her purple Crocs, but the rest of us weren't much better, with Twig in his too small pyjamas, me in Grandma's mint green nightie (it's too pretty to just wear at parties) and Jas in her bikini and sunglasses,

'Because it's so hot,' she explained, 'and because of the sausage smoke.'

The doctor (whose name is Tom Reynolds) peered through the smoke. Grandma glared back. Elsie started sicking up bits of wood under the table. 'Mrs Hanratty told me you fainted,' Dr Reynolds said.

'Mrs Hanratty exaggerates everything,' Grandma said.

'And bumped your head.'

'A tiny knock,' Grandma scoffed, but Dr Reynolds said, 'Even so, Constance, I would like to examine you, preferably somewhere I can actually see you,' and we all followed him out of the kitchen.

Dr Reynolds says Grandma is dehydrated. He says she has been overdoing it, working in her garden and probably running after us. 'I know you think your grandmother is as strong as an ox,' he told us, 'but she had a nasty fall in the spring, and she has to learn to rest.'

Jas said Grandma already has a nap every afternoon. Dr Reynolds said that was wonderful, and well done Grandma. Grandma remarked that she had known Dr Reynolds when he was a small boy, and that he always had very dirty knees.

'What does dehydration mean, exactly?' I asked.

'It means there are not enough fluids in her body,'

Dr Reynolds explained. 'In this heat, we need to keep out of the sun and drink plenty of water. If we don't drink enough, we can get headaches, migraines, become light-headed and even faint. Also, our kidneys can stop working, and that is very serious. Have you studied kidney function in science?'

'They clean your wee,' Twig said.

'Exactly! And if we don't look after our kidneys, ultimately the toxins in our unclean urine can poison us, and it begins to affect our brain.'

'Poisoned by wee!' Jas laughed so hard snot came out of her nose.

'That will be quite enough of that,' Grandma sniffed.

'Two litres of water a day!' Dr Reynolds told her. 'I'm also giving you some rehydration sachets. No gardening, put your feet up, and no running after grandchildren. Let them look after you for a change. Where is David?'

'Whale-watching in New Zealand,' Twig said darkly.

'And Cassie?'

'Baby-watching near Basingstoke,' I said.

Dr Reynolds sighed. I think he's known Mum and Dad for a long time.

'Well, another adult about the place wouldn't be a

bad thing, but you'll have to do,' he told us. 'There's not a lot wrong with her that rest won't cure. I'll call back in a couple of days.'

He wagged his finger at Grandma as he spoke. I thought that she might bite it off.

'Doctors!' she cried when he had gone. 'After I'm dressed, I'm going to see to my tomatoes. Then I will check the ponies with Jas and after that, we will all go to the stream. Don't look at me like that, Blue.'

'He said you should rest.'

'And so I shall. By the stream. When I have done what I have to do. I'm not having young Tom Reynolds telling me what to do.'

I emailed Skye about Elsie. He gave me his address before he went away. I just wanted to know if there was anything we could do to avoid the whole fox poo incident again. Grandma says I don't speak to her with sufficient authority. 'Dogs need a firm hand!' she says. Elsie adores Grandma and does everything she says, but however firm I try to be, she ignores me completely. She wanted to sleep with Grandma, but Grandma says bedrooms are no place for dogs, and that I should take her downstairs to her basket. So right now she is lying on my bed, right across my feet, and I wouldn't mind except she does still smell a bit. I just tried to kick her off, but she growled at me. Then, when I let her stay, I swear she smiled.

Tuesday 5 August, very, very early

It's not even light yet, but I'm awake, and I am so, so scared.

It was too hot by the stream. Grandma said it wasn't but I could see that she was struggling, and when she stood up to go in the water, she stumbled. I didn't really pay attention at the time. She said she'd caught her foot on a stone, but I know now it wasn't that.

Elsie heard her first tonight. She woke me up rolling off the bed and nosed open my door. I went back to sleep, but a few minutes later she was back, whining and tugging at my covers.

'I wish Skye *had* put you in kennels,' I grumbled, but then I heard it.

The music, coming from Grandma's room. Her door was open, and light was spilling into the corridor, and she was singing.

The door to Jas and Twig's room opened and they both shuffled out, half asleep, Jas still tangled in her bed sheet.

'Is there a party or something?' Twig asked.

'Is it ghosts?' Jas said.

'We should go and see,' I said.

But we hesitated. Even before going in, I think we all knew it wasn't right. Grandma often has trouble sleeping, but this was new.

This music.

Elsie ran ahead of us as we crept down the corridor but stopped at the open door.

In her room, Grandma was sitting at her dressing table, wearing a long fur coat over her nightie with a little pillbox hat. She was doing her make-up – Grandma, who only ever wears a tiny bit of pale pink lipstick. I don't know where she found it all. It must have been very old, and she'd done it all wrong, like a little girl playing. Her eyelids were painted blue right up to her eyebrows, and her lips were bright red, and her face was white with powder.

'She looks like a clown at the circus,' Jas whispered.

Elsie was pawing at her lap but Grandma pushed her away. She slunk back towards us, and Jas put her arms round her.

'Hurry!' Grandma cried. 'Or we're going to be late!'

Twig and Jas both nudged me forward.

'Late for what?' I asked.

'Church, of course!'

I glanced over my shoulder. Twig shrugged his shoulders. Jas tightened her arms around the dog.

'Church?' I said.

'For my wedding.' Grandma's voice was high and breathless. 'I'm waiting for Daddy.'

'Why is she talking like that?' Jas asked.

'Is the car here?' Grandma said. 'Did they put the ribbons on it, and the flowers?'

'I don't like it.' Jas's lower lip started to wobble.

Grandma was applying mascara in wild extravagant sweeps, leaving black streaks across her temples.

'Let me do it for you,' I said.

I took a cotton wool pad from the dressing table and started to clean her face.

'You've put on a bit too much,' I said.

Twig stepped up beside me.

'We have to tell her,' he murmured.

'Tell her what?'

'The truth.'

'How?'

Twig knelt down in front of Grandma and took her hands in his.

'I think maybe you are a bit confused,' he said gently. 'Grandma, Grandpa is dead.'

Grandma smiled, the sweetest, loveliest smile.

'How can he be dead, dear?' she asked. 'When we're not even married yet?'

Over by the door, Jas was clinging tight to Elsie. Twig's jaw was set very firm, and my own eyes were stinging.

'He is, Grandma,' I said. 'He died six years ago.'

'Dead?' repeated Grandma.

And then she cried. She cried and cried and cried. I tried to comfort her. I thought we should take the rest of her make-up off and help her back to bed, like maybe she was sleepwalking or having a bad dream or something, but when we tried to make her she sobbed that we should leave her alone.

We crept out, taking Elsie with us.

I should have made her rest this afternoon, like Dr Reynolds said. I have called everyone I can think of. I have left messages for Dr Reynolds in Plumpton, and for Mum near Bath, for Dad in New Zealand and Lizzie in France and even Zoran in Sarajevo. Nobody is answering. We've pushed the beds together in my room and we are all huddled together in them now, including Elsie. Every now and then, I tiptoe down the corridor. The crying has stopped. I peeped in through the door. Grandma was in the armchair by the window and didn't turn around. Jas is asleep, her arms around Elsie. Twig and I are leaning against the headboard, staring out of the door we have left open so we can be sure to hear the phone ring downstairs.

The phone just rang, waking us all up. Twig jumped out of bed and ran to answer it. I went after him.

'Who is it?' I asked.

Twig handed me the phone.

'It's Zoran,' he said. 'He says he's back from Bosnia, and he's on his way.'

It's getting light outside. This is so different from dawn two days ago. There is nothing we can do but wait.

Tuesday 5 August, later

We were all asleep when they arrived. Elsie woke us, barking at the front door. I looked out of the window and there were Zoran and Gloria, both of them, getting out of Gloria's beaten-up old Ford.

I ran downstairs and straight into Zoran's hug. The feel of his beard scratching my cheek was so familiar and safe I didn't want to let go.

'We got here as soon as we could,' he said.

'I thought you were in Sarajevo,' I told him. 'I only called because no one else was answering.'

'He got back last night,' Gloria said. She didn't sound very pleased, but I don't suppose driving nearly three hundred miles to rescue your boyfriend's ex-charges' grandmother on her imaginary wedding day is anybody's idea of a romantic reunion. But then Jas came hurtling downstairs and into Gloria's arms, and Gloria went all soft as she said, 'Hello Jas, I've missed you.'

With her tight black clothes and long dark hair, Gloria may look like a scary warrior princess, but underneath she is the sort of person whose heart melts at the sight of kittens. I think Jas loves her almost as much as Zoran does.

'Take us to your grandmother,' Gloria ordered, and there's something about her – maybe it's all that shouting at people on horseback – you just do what she says. We all fell in line behind her, including Elsie back from a rummage round the garden, and Twig yawning as he staggered out of my bedroom. Even after a long car journey, Gloria looked so regal and perfect, I think we all believed everything would be fine just because she wanted it to be.

Grandma was lying on her bed now, still wearing

her fur coat and with her crazy make-up all smudged, but fast asleep and looking so peaceful that the scenes from last night seemed quite impossible. Her eyelids fluttered open and she smiled the sweetest smile, one I've never seen before that made her look younger somehow and less formidable.

'You're awake!' Jas ran up to the bed.

For a moment – a good moment, when I still thought everything was fine – she looked confused. Her face cleared as she recognised us, and she smiled and said, 'Zoran, dear, nice to see you! Have you come to visit? And you have brought your lovely Gloria.'

And I knew immediately that things were still all wrong, because there is no way in a million years Grandma would ever, *ever* allow Zoran to see her in her nightie, looking the way she did. Zoran advanced towards the bed and took her hand.

'I overslept,' she told him. 'We'll have to hurry, Caspian will be waiting.'

'Who is Caspian?' Gloria whispered to me.

'My grandfather,' I said.

'He's dead,' Twig explained.

'I don't know where Daddy is,' Grandma said.

Gloria ushered us out of the room and into the kitchen while she called the ambulance.

I think Elsie knows something bad is happening. She sat with us while we waited, quieter than I have ever seen her. When the paramedics brought Grandma downstairs, Elsie trotted out after them, and stuck her muzzle into Grandma's hand.

Grandma bent to scratch Elsie behind the ears and stroke her head and kiss her on the nose.

'Good dog,' she said. 'We'll be back right after church.'

She straightened up and beamed. 'A perfect day for a wedding,' she said.

'Shall we get in the ambulance, dear?' said one of the paramedics. Grandma frowned.

'Who the hell are you?' she asked.

Zoran followed them to the hospital in the Land Rover. I asked if I could go too, but he told me to stay. Elsie is still sitting out there now, in the exact spot where Grandma got into the ambulance. Twig says he tried to move her, but she won't budge.

It's later now.

Zoran says the doctors have sedated Grandma and put her on a drip to rehydrate her, and also that she is on antibiotics because her kidneys did become infected, and that this has affected her brain.

'So she is being poisoned,' Twig said. 'Just like Dr Reynolds said. And the poison is making her mad. Like mercury, or arsenic, or lead poisoning.'

'But it's reversible,' Zoran assured us. 'Once the infection goes, she will be absolutely fine.'

Mum called. She asked whether should she come down, but Zoran said we would call her tomorrow with more news. Lizzie rang too, offering to come back from France. Zoran, who had no idea who she was, said no.

'She had a message for you,' he frowned. 'Something about the sky saying hello, and sorry about the fox poo but she loves it, and hose her down the best you can.'

'Nothing else?' I asked, and Zoran said he thought that was probably quite enough already. We've tried calling Dad, but his phone is off.

It would have been the nicest day ever if we hadn't been so worried about Grandma. I don't mean that to sound unfeeling, because we *did* worry about her. But after Zoran arrived, nice things started to happen.

'We have ponies,' Jas told Gloria.

'So I heard,' Gloria said.

Even though she looks after horses for a living, I have never thought of Gloria as anything other than a town person. Her stables are tiny and crammed underneath the motorway and next to a railway line, her clothes are a town person's clothes, she talks like a Londoner. But it turns out she is a perfect country person too. She took her boots off the minute we showed her the stream and paddled. She knows even more bird names than Twig does. She raced Marigold bareback round the field. She wheeled a barrow full of horse manure up to the potager. She showed us how to dig it into the soil. She found the first ripe red tomatoes in the greenhouse. She made us dig a fire pit in the field and gather wood for burning.

Then Zoran discovered Grandpa's piano when he came back from the hospital. It hasn't been tuned for years because Grandma doesn't play, but he said it was one of the loveliest instruments he'd ever seen. He played for ages, working his way through the dusty stack of old sheet music that has sat on top of the piano for as long as I can remember, while we drove into Plumpton with Gloria to buy food to cook over the fire pit, sausages and burgers and marshmallows. We started the fire in the early evening, and ate just as it was starting to get dark, sitting on the grass and burning our fingers, with juice from the meat trickling down our chins and

Elsie watching like a hawk in case we dropped anything.

'I could get used to this,' Zoran said, and Gloria said she could too.

There was ice cream for pudding which we ate with the last strawberries from the potager, and a bottle of wine which Gloria drank with Zoran. With her long dark hair and her cheeks flushed, barefoot in the grass, Jas says she looked like a beautiful gypsy. Zoran never took his eyes off her. Then after we'd eaten, when it was quite dark, we went to check on the ponies and Twig said to Gloria, 'It's still so warm. Why don't you take Zoran to look at the stream?'

Jas said, 'Let's all go for a midnight paddle!' and then she said 'Ouch' because Twig kicked her in the shins.

'I'd love a midnight swim,' I said. 'I can't believe we've never done it before.'

'If *you* go down to the stream,' Twig said, 'Elsie will want to swim, and then you will spend the whole night trying to dry her before she sleeps on your bed. Only Zoran and Gloria should go.'

Twig turned towards them, blocking Jas and me, and spoke to them in an oddly formal voice. 'You will see that it's very, very pretty there. Do walk on the bridge. That's where you get the nicest view.'

Jas said, 'Oh!' and Twig kicked her again. She clapped her hand over her mouth, but Zoran and Gloria didn't even notice, because they were already walking away hand in hand towards the stream.

Above them, in a perfect starlit sky, hung a perfect full round moon.

The Film Diaries of
Bluebell Gadsby

Scene Eleven
The Geriatric Ward

INTERIOR. DAY.

A quiet room in a small town hospital.
It's a beautiful day again, but the
windows are all closed. The swing
doors onto the ward are operated by
security buttons. No one can enter or
leave who is not supposed to. This
makes it feel like a prison.

Twelve hospital beds, the kind with
wheels that can be raised up or down,
with plastic under white hospital
sheets. Lockers beside each bed,
curtains on rails around them to make
pretend rooms, though most of them are
open anyway.

In each bed lies an old person. They

all look the same - pale, grey, and like they have somehow shrunk. Their hair is thin, their skin like paper, pulled tight over their bones. All are dozing, with the exception of one old lady in a pink knitted wrap and even pinker lipstick, who is eating sweets and reading a magazine.

It smells of detergent, old people and pee.

In a bed at the end of the ward, GRANDMA is beginning to look like them. She is asleep, her mouth slightly open, her hands folded over the covers. Her breath is shallow. A drip stands by her bed, its plastic tube attached to the needle taped in her arm. Zoran explains that the other tube, the one that goes under the covers, is to take her wee away.

A NURSE approaches, looking annoyed.

NURSE
What are you doing? You can't film in here. Turn that thing off right now.

CAMERAMAN (BLUE) lowers camera but keeps it running, so that sound is still recorded. She can't look the nurse in the eye. She doesn't want to look at anyone or anything, unless it's through the camera. Behind her, JASMINE and TWIG can't take their eyes off Grandma.

                    ZORAN
                   (gently)
     They are here to visit their
grandmother, Constance Gadsby. Nurse,
    they are upset. The filming – it
   helps her. I can promise the film
     will not be seen by anyone, in
    fact I guarantee that I myself will
                 destroy it.

           OLD LADY IN PINK WRAP
          (cackles, off camera)
Oh, let the girl film, Nora! I always
     fancied myself as a movie star.

GRANDMA
(waking up, also off camera)
Caspian? Is that you?

ZORAN
I'm afraid Caspian couldn't come
today, Constance.

GRANDMA
Where is Mr Pigeon?

OLD LADY IN PINK WRAP
Who's blinking Mr Pigeon when
he's at home?

ZORAN
(low, aside)
He is her dog. At least, he was. Mr
Pigeon is actually dead.
(louder, to Grandma)
Mr Pigeon is off chasing rabbits.
Perhaps I'll bring him tomorrow.

Grandma goes back to sleep.

OLD LADY IN PINK WRAP
(calls for Nora)
Nora! Nora! If this old nutter can
have her dead dog in here, I want my
cat! Do you hear me? I want my Tabby,
and I want her NOW!

When another old lady started to shout that she wanted her budgie, Zoran took the camera out of my hands and announced that it was time to go.

'We'll come back tomorrow.'

Jas said she never wanted to go back, ever. Zoran said that was all right too.

'Grandma looks like she's going to die,' Jas said.

'She doesn't look well,' Zoran admitted. 'But I promise she is not going to die. In fact, she is already a lot better.'

'If she's a lot better,' Twig asked, 'how come she's still mad?'

Zoran said that probably she was just tired, but he didn't look very convinced.

Mum says we have to go home. Zoran called her when we got back from the hospital. 'Constance is receiving excellent care,' he said, and Mum replied that was very good, and perhaps it would be easier for everyone now if we just went back to London.

'But we can't!' I cried. They all turned to look at me, and I blushed. 'We have to look after Elsie. We promised Skye.'

'And there's the garden,' Twig said. 'We can't just leave it. Grandma's spent so long looking after it.'

'Jas?' Zoran asked. 'Surely you want to go home and see your little brother?'

Jas's lower lip wobbled as she said, 'We have to take care of Marigold and Hester as well.'

'And we can't very well leave Constance,' Zoran said.

'Will you stay with us?' I asked him.

Zoran looked up at Gloria. She shook her head, just a tiny bit, so you almost couldn't see it. Zoran frowned.

'Of course I'll stay,' he said.

This morning Gloria found an old pair of jodhpurs that used to belong to Grandma, the sort they had before Lycra was invented, with narrow legs and a wide bottom. Most people just look a really odd shape in them, but obviously not Gloria. They made her look like a splendid and even scarier riding-mistress from the 1940s or something, when it was all right to beat children with riding crops. She glared at Zoran. He didn't look away.

'As long as you need me,' he said.

Gloria marched off towards the paddock. A few minutes later, we saw her riding Marigold out towards the moor.

They quarrelled in the kitchen when she came

back. We crowded round outside the door and listened.

'I don't understand why you're so angry,' Zoran was saying.

'I'm angry because all that family has to do is click their fingers and you come running.'

'Is that family us?' Jas whispered.

'I'm afraid so,' I murmured back.

'They need me!' Zoran pleaded. 'Gloria, Constance is ill, there's no one here, we can't just abandon her in hospital!'

'*I* need you. Zoran, you've been away for ages, we need to talk.'

'Soon,' Zoran promised.

'Where is David? Why can't Cassie come down? Why is it always, *always* you who ends up looking after everybody?'

'I don't know! Because I care?'

We all followed her out when she came down with her bags. She kissed each of us, and said she hoped Grandma would be better soon, then she got into her car without talking to Zoran.

We stepped back as he put his hand on her door.

'Please stay,' we heard him say, and also, 'I love you, Gloria. Please don't go.'

Gloria looked at him really sadly then, and said

that unlike him, she had responsibilities, and that riding schools didn't run themselves. 'It's called real life,' she said. 'And it's not something you're terribly good at.'

She pulled her door shut. Zoran stepped back. She started the engine.

'This is your grandfather's village all over again,' she told him.

Zoran kicked a tree stump, swore, then spent the afternoon playing the piano. Twig gardened. I sat in the hall to write. Jas stood in the doorway between the hall and the living room and said that she was bored.

'Why don't you make a get well card for your grandmother?' Zoran said, not looking up from his music.

Jas said that was the sort of thing you said to little children to make them shut up. Zoran carried on playing.

'Or write her a poem,' I suggested.

Jas said to forget it, and that she had a better idea. A few minutes later I saw her march past the front door towards the paddock, carrying Grandma's gardening hat and a pair of scissors.

Zoran crashed out a few chords and closed the lid of the piano.

'It's no good,' he said. 'I can't concentrate.'

I left the hall and went to lie on the sofa.

'Why is Gloria so cross?' I asked.

Zoran said it was grown-up stuff that I wouldn't understand.

'That's quite rude,' I said.

He opened the piano again and played a moody scale.

'Is it because you won't move in with her?' I asked.

His hands crashed down onto the keyboard.

'This family!' he said. 'How do you know about that?'

'Flora,' I shrugged. 'She always knows everything. She says you have commitment issues.'

'Yes, well. Flora would.'

'What did Gloria mean, it's just like your grandfather's village?' I asked, and Zoran rubbed his face for ages, which is something I've noticed him do more and more when he doesn't know how to answer.

'She means I don't belong there,' he said.

'Why not? You looked so happy in the photograph, you and your sister by the well.'

'The village does not exist,' Zoran said. 'It was destroyed during the war. The well is all that's left.'

You forget sometimes that photographs only tell part of a story.

Zoran started to pick out a tune on the piano with one finger.

'I recognise that,' I said.

'Do you?'

'What is it?'

Jas appeared and said she needed my camera.

'That's the tune Gloria's dad always used to whistle,' she said.

'My camera's upstairs,' I told her, and she charged off again.

'You do belong here though,' I told Zoran. 'With us. You're part of the family.'

He rubbed his face again. I hugged him. Jas sprinted past the door, holding my camera.

'What do you want it for?' I shouted.

'Nothing!'

'It *is* something.' Twig wandered in barefoot from the garden, cramming a handful of raspberries in his mouth. 'It's hilarious, but I'm not sure Grandma's going to like it.'

'It's to remind Grandma of her honeymoon!' Jas cried when we went out after her.

In the photos I took this afternoon, Twig is laughing his head off, his face stained red with raspberry juice. Zoran has his face in his hands and is trying to look disapproving, but I can tell he's trying not to laugh as well. There's Marigold with a crown of daisy chains. Elsie with a red ribbon round her neck and fat Hester looking magnificent, dappled coat shining, hooves polished, tail and mane plaited and on her head, with holes cut out for her ears and secured by a long silk scarf, Grandma's favourite gardening hat.

There is absolutely nothing to suggest that anything is wrong.

Friday 8 August

Elsie is pining, and nobody can sleep.

She spends her days sitting in the exact same spot as on the day they took Grandma away. When I bring her in at night, she cries. The first night Grandma was in hospital, she wouldn't stop scratching at her bedroom door, but when I let her in all she did was howl. Zoran locked her in the kitchen. When we came down in the morning she'd weed all over the floor. Now at night I leave all the doors open hoping she'll find somewhere to settle, but she just wanders from room to room, fretting and whining and keeping us all awake. I've emailed Skye to ask what to do about that now too. I had no idea dog care could be so difficult.

We have been banned from seeing Grandma 'until further notice', Nora has said to Zoran. He went yesterday and today but until she is completely better, Nora says, 'Granny needs peace and quiet.' Jas has changed her mind about never wanting to set foot in the hospital again, and says it isn't fair.

'We would be quiet as mice,' she said.

'No,' Zoran said.

'Teeny tiny baby mice.'

'She's been sedated anyway. She wouldn't even know you were there.'

'I'm sure she would,' Twig grumbled behind Zoran's back. 'She would *sense* us.'

It was a bit less hot this afternoon, and I took Elsie for a walk on the moor. She wouldn't come at first. She lay under Grandma's deckchair by the potager wall and actually growled at me. I only got her out by bribing her with dog treats, but once we were out in open country, with fewer reminders of Skye and Grandma, she perked up and started to run around.

It's different, walking with a dog. Grandma

and Grandpa had others, of course, but we were little, always with Grandma or Grandpa. This was the first time of it being just me and a dog and it felt . . . grown-up. Like it wasn't just about me, because I was responsible for someone else, and that someone was looking after me too, running off and then back again, to check I was still there. We walked for ages. We splashed in tiny streams, and lay in the heather, and I got a little bit sunburned because I forgot to put on sun cream, and it was only as I came back towards Horsehill at the end of the afternoon, and saw Grandma's funny twisted tree, that I realised I hadn't thought about Iris at all.

This is what Skye has done, with his sunrise and his dog.

Dartmoor used to be all about her. Iris running, Iris shouting, Iris making up games. But without me even noticing, time has moved on. Skye has shown me a side to this place that she will never see.

And I'm not sure I like that. I'm not sure I'm ready for it.

When Jas isn't with the ponies, doing Skye's daily chores, exercising them and practising her riding, she is writing. She says her poem has become very dark and tragic, because she has included all the bits about the hospital and the crazy people wanting their pets, and also descriptions of Grandma. She wants Pumpkin to know everything, but she is starting to get a bit tired of it.

'Why isn't Mum here?' she asked this evening at dinner. 'Then Pumpkin could see everything in person.'

And I think at last I understand.

If Mum comes here with Pumpkin, Horsehill will become about him. In time, the living Pumpkin will replace the dead Iris. And maybe she's not ready for that either.

So we wait: for Mum to overcome her sorrow, and for Grandma to improve, for the boys to come back from France. Twig works in the potager – it is his domain, just as the ponies are Jas's and Elsie is mine – and waits for tomatoes to ripen. Slowly, the wilderness is taking over. However hard he works, Twig can't stop the sun from baking the grass, roses from turning to brambles, weeds and wild flowers from blowing in. His hands are permanently earthy. Jas's hair looks like the manes of the wild ponies, with bits of straw and briar caught in its long dark tangles. The sun has turned her skin a deep coppery colour which makes her dark eyes look almost black, and her dress is even more torn than when we arrived, and suddenly too short. I have taken to walking barefoot, like Twig, and in just a few days my soles have hardened and cracked.

The days drift by to the sound of Zoran's piano. There is still no news from Dad. Zoran keeps trying to contact him, but Mum says Dad warned her he would be off grid for a week, looking at his whales. Someone has to come, because I think Zoran has to go back to London. There has been another argument with Gloria, but since then he hasn't heard from her either. And so he visits Grandma, and cares for us and the house, and plays for hours, but he is waiting also, waiting for his life to start again, with Gloria, away from us.

Skye replied. He says I should try wrapping Elsie in something of Grandma's, a blanket or a sweater or shawl. He says the smell might comfort her. I suggested her old grey cashmere cardigan, the one she wears all the time with the holes in the elbows, and he said that sounded perfect.

I thought about telling him about our walk, about how it made me feel, seeing things differently, through new eyes – his eyes, I suppose. But it seemed strange, to put things like that in an email. Then I asked how things were going in France and he said good, but he misses Horsehill, and that they'd be back exactly a week tomorrow and I sent a smiley, and then I logged off because really, a smiley? I'm turning into Flora.

Ollie hasn't been in touch at all, but I've been looking at my film of our day at New Bridge. I can't believe it was only last week. I can't believe what I did that day, either. In the video, Ollie is always laughing, and it's like he's casting a spell on me all over again.

Saturday 9 August, very early in the morning

It's a little after midnight, and I just woke up with a huge jump. I don't know how that happens, how you can be completely asleep one minute and wide awake the next, with a thought so obvious you don't know how you ever missed it.

The sooner Dad gets here, the sooner Zoran can go back to London to sort things out with Gloria.

Obviously.

And the only person nobody has contacted about Grandma is Flora. Which is 1) very wrong, because Flora loves Grandma and 2) *really* stupid, because right now she is the closest person to Dad.

So I got out of bed and went downstairs to write

to her. In my message, I decided to be as dramatic as I possibly could, because basically Flora responds to drama like a vampire does to blood.

'Grandma is in hospital,' I wrote. 'They have put her on a drip. She is surrounded by corpses and will surely die herself.'

It took Flora about two minutes to respond.

```
9/08, 11:36
FLORA GADSBY
Oh my God!
```

```
9/08, 11:36
FLORA GADSBY
Seriously, corpses?
```

```
9/08, 11:37
FLORA GADSBY
Can she not be saved?
```

```
9/08, 11:37
BLUEBELL GADSBY
She is suffering from acute dehydration
and infection of the kidneys. Tell Dad
he must come at once. Where are the
whales?
```

```
9/08, 11:38
FLORA GADSBY
Miles  away!  Like,  days.  I'll  leave
right now!
```

```
9/08, 11:38
BLUEBELL GADSBY
Can you? What about work?
```

```
9/08, 11:39
FLORA GADSBY
They won't miss me. All I do is sit
around  anyway.  I'll  get  Dad  home,
don't you worry.
```

I peeped into the kitchen on my way upstairs and smiled at the sight of Elsie fast asleep in her basket, Grandma's cashmere cardigan torn to shreds.

By 11:42, I was back in bed.

Saturday 9 August (ctd)

'Please go and do something,' Zoran begged me this morning at breakfast. 'If I see you drooping about one more minute, I will throw you in the stream.'

'I do not droop!' I said.

'Yes, you do. When you're not sighing or staring into space or grinning like a maniac, you droop. Anyone would think you were in love rather than desperately worried.'

'In love?' Jas said. 'With Ollie?'

'I am not in love with anyone,' I said. But even so, I grabbed my bike and escaped.

The stream at Melisandra's pool has gone down too. It doesn't look nearly as inviting as it did before. I walked up the hill to the old stone village Twig explored with Skye, and I stood on the bridge looking down at the pool itself, which still wasn't turquoise but green and murky, with water flies and other bugs skimming the surface, and then I sat on the beach for ages in my swimming costume, working up the courage to go in.

It's dark under that bridge, and it *is* scary, especially when the water is so low you can feel weeds brushing your tummy as you swim and there's no one else around to egg you on, but I did it.

I almost wished for Iris, as usual. Then I thought of Jas, and almost wished for Mum and Pumpkin to come. I almost wished for Skye and Ollie to come back, and for Ollie to like me as much as I like him.

But wishes are precious, and you have to think

carefully before you make them, especially if there may be a witch listening, and so I made the only wish that matters right now.

I wished for Grandma to be better.

I swam right out into the middle to prove I wasn't afraid and I swear there was this moment, as I flipped onto my back and wished out loud, when the sun broke through the trees and the water turned not blue, but golden.

Lizzie called this evening for news of Grandma, and I talked to Skye.

'How's Elsie?' he asked.

I told him about Elsie shredding Grandma's cardigan.

'But it's working,' I said. 'She's much happier.'

'How is your Grandma?'

'A bit better, I hope. We're not allowed to see her. Can I ask you a dumb question? Melisandra's pool. Do you think it works?'

He didn't answer for a bit, and I worried he thought I really was stupid.

'Do you think there really is a ghost at Satan's Tor?' he asked at last.

'It feels like there might be,' I admitted.

'So,' he said. And then, 'I bet it does come true.'

I wanted to ask after Ollie, but I didn't know how without appearing too obvious, like what I was really asking was 'Has he talked about me?' Instead I said, 'Send my love to everyone,' and Skye just said, 'Sure.'

Monday 11 August

Grandma has been in hospital nearly a week. Today, they finally allowed us to go back. It was much calmer than the first time we went, but still horrible.

Nora was on duty again. When she saw us I thought she wasn't going to let us in, but she just said, 'I won't have you disturbing the old dears', and we tiptoed in.

Someone came out of a side door as we entered the ward. Voices blared out. 'The day room,' Nora explained when we asked. 'They watch TV.'

'Is Grandma in there?' Jas skipped over to look before Nora could answer, and stopped dead in her tracks.'

'Oh,' I said, joining her, and 'Oh,' Twig agreed.

There were lots of old people sitting in the day room. The TV was on full blast but none of them were watching, even the ones sitting right in front of it. Most of them were asleep, I think, with their heads drooping forward over their chests. One old lady was dribbling, and an old man was clawing at his pyjamas, trying to pull them off while a nurse tried to stop him.

'It's back to bed if you can't behave!' she scolded him.

'It's horrible,' Jas said.

'Like a vision of hell,' Twig agreed.

'Does Grandma come here?' I asked Nora.

'Your granny's in her bed,' said Nora. 'And it is *not* a vision of hell.'

Grandma was asleep. They've taken away the tubes, but she has a bruise on her arm where the drip went in. Her infection has completely gone now and she is fully hydrated, but I have never seen anyone look so ill. Her suntan has faded, and her dark grey hair is lighter, and she's lost weight so that her skin looks like the other old people's, stretched over her bones.

'She still needs rest,' Nora warned.

I didn't think Grandma was awake at all the whole time we were there. We sat round, whispering and wondering if we ought to be talking to her even though she couldn't hear us, like they do on TV to people who are dying and unconscious, and their relatives start to confess things like 'It was me who murdered your guinea pig' or 'I am your real father'.

But none of us had anything to confess, except for Jas about the gardening hat and she said she would rather not admit to that just in case Grandma actually heard.

The doctor came. He read Grandma's notes and said he'd like to keep her in for a few more days.

'But I thought her infection was better,' I said.

The doctor said it was, but you could never be too careful with old people.

Jas whispered, loudly, that Grandma looked even worse now than when she went into hospital. Twig said he'd read somewhere that people do get sick in hospitals, because of superbugs that multiply wherever there are diseases. Nora bristled and said, 'Not on my ward.'

'Believe me,' said the doctor. 'Granny is better off here.'

Grandma's eyes fluttered and the doctor leaned over to speak to her. 'Aren't you better off here, Mrs Gadsby?' he said right in her face.

'I want to go home,' Grandma murmured.

'You see?' Twig cried.

Zoran told us all to be quiet and asked the doctor what would happen if Grandma were to come home.

'She needs constant attention and care,' the doctor said.

'We can do that!' I said.

'She really is better off here,' the doctor said.

'But why?' I asked, and Zoran said that was enough.

'We'll leave you to say goodbye,' Nora said.

She hurried off after the doctor. Jas stuck her tongue out behind her back, then Twig screamed as Grandma's hand shot out and grabbed him by the wrist.

Nora hurried back. Grandma's bright blue eyes were wide and staring, and she had a little bit of dribble trickling out of her mouth like the old lady in the TV room.

'Out!' said Nora.

'Take me home,' Grandma hissed. 'Or I will *never* forgive you.'

'*Why* can't she come home?' Jas asked Zoran in the car. 'If she's better, why does she have to stay?'

'The doctor wants her to rest.'

'She can rest at home,' I told him. 'We can look after her. She shouldn't be there, Zoran. She's not like those other people. Grandma needs . . .' I paused, thinking of what Grandma needed. 'She needs her garden, and the smell of roses and the moor, and Elsie doing crazy things and her own bedroom. It's not about doctors and nurses, it's about what she loves. I actually think she might die if she stays in there.'

Jas started to cry and said she knew exactly what it feels like to want to go home. I reached through the dog guard into the back of the Land Rover and took her hand. On the bench opposite her, Twig sat rubbing his wrist and looking out of the window.

'What do you think?' I asked him.

He dragged his gaze slowly away from the view and towards me.

'It's like a curse,' he said.

'We're cursed!' Jas sobbed.

'She said she would never forgive us.'

'Please tell the doctor she should come home,' I pleaded with Zoran.

'You are being melodramatic,' Zoran scolded us. He glanced over his shoulder. The car swerved to the left and nearly came off the road. We all screamed. Zoran pulled hard to the right and a truck thundered past with its horn blaring. 'We are perfectly safe,' Zoran said, but his voice was shaking. 'Melodrama is the true curse of this family. Sometimes you just have to accept that grown-ups know best. Now let's talk about something else. Like this wretched car with its terrible steering.' He started to go on about what a nightmare the Land Rover was to drive and how it always pulls to left, like our near brush with death wasn't his fault. 'It ought to be scrapped!' he said, but nobody was listening.

I think Zoran knows we're cross with him, because after we had lunch we didn't see him for the rest of the day. He spent the whole afternoon at the piano. He says that he is composing a sonata.

Elsie is completely back on form and spent the afternoon digging up a flower bed of Grandma's favourite tulip bulbs, then running away from me when I took her out on the moor, which means that I spent most of the afternoon tramping across the countryside yelling at her. When I finally got her home, Twig and Jas were sitting in the Land Rover, waiting for me.

'No,' I said.

'We have to,' said Twig.

'Think of the curse,' urged Jas.

I tried to explain why we couldn't do what they wanted. I said it was dangerous, and irresponsible, and that we would get into trouble. I hit them with every sensible argument I could think of and they refused to listen.

'If you won't help us,' Jas said, 'we will just go ahead without you.'

'You can't go ahead without me,' I said.

'Then you have to help us,' Twig said.

'I could tell Zoran.'

'You wouldn't!' Jas gasped.

'You're right,' I admitted. 'I wouldn't.'

And so everything is ready. The Land Rover has cushions, food, water, blankets. We've rehearsed our parts until we know them by heart. Now all we have to do is execute the plan.

Tomorrow we rescue Grandma.

Tuesday 12 August

We made Zoran take us to the hospital first thing in the morning, because that is always when Grandma is strongest. Then, as soon as we arrived, Jas announced that she needed the toilet and please would Zoran wait for her.

Grandma was sitting up in bed reading a magazine when we arrived, and I could tell at once that she was feeling a lot better than yesterday. She'd done her hair and she glared at us like I imagine Melisandra would have glared at her executioners when they came to drown her.

'No sign of a reprieve then,' she said.

'Can you walk?' Twig asked.

'Of course I can walk,' Grandma snapped.

'What was the date of your wedding?'

'I beg your pardon?'

'Please just answer the question,' I begged.

'17th June 1966.'

I didn't want to ask the next question, but Twig insisted. He said we had to know if Grandma had fully reversed.

'When did Grandpa die?' Twig asked.

'23rd November 2008,' Grandma said. 'World War Two ended on 8th May 1945. In Europe. In Asia it ended on 15th August. George VI died on 6th February 1952 and *Sergeant Pepper's Lonely Hearts Club Band* was released in 1967. What else do you want, my credit card details?'

'Here comes Jas,' said Twig. 'Without Zoran.'

Jas limped towards us, looking droopy.

'You're overdoing it,' I hissed.

'Zoran's gone to buy me a Coke,' Jas said. 'I told him I felt sick and it would make me better.'

'Good thinking,' said Twig, and Operation Rescue Grandma began.

The Film Diaries of Bluebell Gadsby

Scene Twelve
(had I filmed it, which I obviously couldn't)
Operation Rescue Grandma

INTERIOR. DAY. THE GERIATRIC WARD AT
ST OSWALD'S HOSPITAL.

                    TWIG
            (assuming the manner of
              a wartime spy)
We must hurry. There isn't much time.
  Grandma, do exactly what we say.

                  GRANDMA
Not until you tell me what's going on.

                  JASMINE
              You have to!

BLUEBELL
Shh, Zoran's coming!

JASMINE
(clutches her tummy, groans and
falls to her knees)
Agh, it hurts!

NORA
(miraculously appearing)
What is going on?

ZORAN
(looking sceptical)
The child appears to be ill.

NORA
Not on my ward!

JASMINE
I think I have appendicitis.

NORA
I will show you the way
to paediatrics.

Nora, Zoran and Jasmine all leave.
Twig waits until they are out of sight,
then pulls the curtains round the bed
and hands Blue an empty rucksack.

TWIG

Shove her valuables in here. Grandma,
put on some outdoor clothes, but
keep your nightie. We don't want them
getting suspicious.

GRANDMA

Suspicious of *what*?

TWIG

We're kidnapping you.

Twig leaves. Grandma beams and starts
issuing instructions.

GRANDMA

Leave the toothbrush! Take the face
cream! Brush my hair and get my pearls!

Twig returns, looking angelic, pushing
a wheelchair and trailing a nurse.

TWIG

Grandma, the nice nurse says we can
take you outside for some fresh air.
She says, just for a few minutes, but
that's all right, isn't it?

GRANDMA
(assuming her most idiotic
expression)
Oh yes, dear. Lovely!

BLUEBELL
(trying to look as angelic as Twig)
Are you well wrapped up? Here, let me
help you into this nice wheelchair.

NURSE
Are you sure you don't want someone
to come with you?

TWIG
Oh, we'll be all right. You're so
busy, and we'll only go as far as the
little garden. We won't even cross
the road. Thank you so much for
your help.

Nurse beams, like she never knew such polite boys existed. Twig, Bluebell and Grandma depart, looking nonchalant. As soon as they leave the ward, they pick up speed. As they make for the main exit, Twig pulls a can of Fanta from the rucksack, shakes it vigorously and hands it to Blue.

TWIG

You know what to do.

Bluebell pauses on the hospital steps and pulls the ring tab on the can. Sticky orange liquid explodes everywhere. Bluebell screams. All eyes - of patients, relatives, orderlies, receptionists, a passing postman and a man delivering flowers - turn upon her. Twig and Grandma disappear at a brisk trot towards the car park.

I made a big thing of trying to clean the floor with a tissue and then with some paper towels from the Ladies. By the time a cleaner arrived with a mop, people had lost interest in me. I bolted for Paediatrics, where Jas and Zoran were sitting on plastic chairs waiting to see a doctor, Jas still clutching her tummy and moaning.

'Are you going to be long?' I asked. 'Only Grandma's asleep and we want to go.'

Zoran said, 'Blue, your sister is seriously ill.'

Jas said, 'Actually, I am feeling much better.'

Twig met us at the entrance to Paediatrics.

'I should say goodbye to Constance,' Zoran said.

'She's sleeping,' Twig told him.

'Nora told us to leave,' I added.

'I want to go home,' Jas whined.

Zoran sighed and said, 'Fine, let's go.'

We were a bit scared Grandma might have another fit or collapse or something, but I don't know any grandmother as amazing as her. It is definitely lucky she's so small though, and also that the Land Rover is so messy. We piled the back with cushions and blankets last night. If Zoran asked, Jas was going to complain about how boring the drive to the hospital was and that she wanted to pretend she was a dog and sleep on the floor. But he didn't even notice, just as he didn't notice, as we climbed back into the Land Rover, that there was a Grandma-shaped lump curled up on the cushions under the blanket.

The drive out of town felt like the longest in my life, especially as Zoran kept saying things like 'Why don't we stop in town for lunch,' or 'It might be a good idea to do a big supermarket shop.'

'Jas has tummy ache,' I said, and 'We can get everything we need in Plumpton.'

'It hardly seems worth the drive,' Zoran said. 'We were only at the hospital about five minutes.'

He stopped on the outskirts of town saying we needed petrol. Jas and Twig pulled faces at him through the back window, blocking it completely so he couldn't see in. Zoran stuck his head back in the driver's door to pick up his wallet.

'Anyone want anything from the shop?' he asked before going to pay.

'No thank you!' we chorused.

'You can sit up for a bit,' I told Grandma when he'd gone. She emerged from under the blankets, beaming. I swear her cheeks were pinker already, and I'm sure it's not just because of the heat.

Twig and Jas made monkey noises to distract

Zoran when he came back, because Grandma wasn't very quick about hiding again. Zoran told them they were savages, and they made even more noise. I put the radio on as loud as it would go, and we all tried not to giggle when he complained.

'That was a horrible drive,' he announced when we got home. 'I don't know what's got into you all today, but I want you to know that I don't like it.'

'Let's go and find Elsie in the kitchen,' I said to soothe him. 'And make a nice cup of tea.'

Grandma almost made it all the way up to her room, but Zoran saw her from the kitchen as she was crossing the hall. He yelled 'Constance!' so loudly that everyone jumped, but by then it was too late.

Everyone is furious with us. Zoran says we have made a fool out of him and he doesn't know why he bothers. The hospital called and shouted quite a lot, then Doctor Reynolds came to the house and got cross with Grandma.

Grandma, who has spent the afternoon eating toast and drinking tea in bed, with her window wide open and Elsie beside her, says that she has never felt better (apparently dogs *are* allowed in bedrooms if you are ill). Dr Reynolds took her temperature and her pulse, looked into her eyes with those torch things they have, and said the district nurse would come tomorrow.

'Kidnapped!' he scolded.

'I'm not going back,' Grandma warned him.

'You are thoroughly irresponsible,' he said. I think Grandma took it as a compliment.

It's quite hard to tell if Dr Reynolds is smiling because he has a beard, but I think that secretly he really likes Grandma. I heard him tell Zoran she was a 'remarkable old lady'. They talked for quite a long time, but when Zoran saw that I was listening he waved me away, and the two of them walked off towards the cars so that I couldn't hear.

The Film Diaries of Bluebell Gadsby

Scene Thirteen
The Sick Room

INTERIOR. DAYTIME.

GRANDMA's bedroom is full of things associated with patients – a bunch of wild flowers crammed into a jug, a wicker basket containing packets of medicine, an army of miniature bottles of mineral water lined up on the bedside table, together with a bunch of grapes and a hand-drawn 'get-well soon' card.

JASMINE wears a pale blue dress of Grandma's, held up by safety pins and bunched under a white apron tied tightly at her waist. She has a red shawl across her shoulders and a white tea towel on her head. She busies around tidying, making tea from a kettle in the corner, arranging biscuits on a plate and occasionally announcing that it's time to take Grandma's temperature. Grandma, who is sitting up in bed playing backgammon with TWIG, refuses to let her.

In an armchair in the corner, ZORAN works on the score of his sonata.

GRANDMA
(having, yet again, lost to Twig)
I would like to get up now.

ZORAN
(not taking his eyes off his score)
The doctor said rest.

GRANDMA
I'm hungry!

ZORAN
Then I will bring you lunch.

He rises and crosses the room. He

pauses at the door, his hand on the
key in the lock.

GRANDMA
Don't you dare lock me in!

ZORAN
(calmly)
Don't you dare try to get out.

Grandma, grumbling, orders Twig to set
up the board for another game. It soon
becomes apparent that, downstairs,
Zoran has failed to make it past the
piano to the kitchen. For once, he is
not working on his sonata (he has left
the score in his armchair). Instead,
he has gone back to Grandpa's stack of
old sheet music.

GRANDMA
(sighs)
Ah, Chopin ...

She leans back against her pillows,
everything else forgotten. Piano music

echoes through the house. Grandma closes her eyes and smiles, the same sweet smile as the night she went mad, when she thought it was her wedding day.

On the floor, at the foot of the bed, Elsie's ears twitch as she sleeps.

Dad called this afternoon, just as I was coming back in from the garden, and he was not in a good mood.

'What on earth is going on?' he demanded. 'I come off the whale boat to find Flora's left the set *with Brandon Taylor* and they're chasing me round the island to tell me your grandmother is allegedly *dying*. Then I speak to Tom Reynolds who tells me she ran away from hospital!'

'She didn't exactly run away . . .'

'*Brandon Taylor*! Hollywood's biggest heartthrob, vanishes because your sister wants him to drive her around! The whole production team are furious!'

'Yes well I'm sorry about . . .'

'Who is looking after your grandmother? Why are you still there? How ill is she? Let me talk to her!'

'I think she's asleep.'

'It's the middle of the day!'

'She's tired, Dad.'

'I'm not surprised she's tired!'

'Oh look, here's Zoran.'

Poor Zoran. He came downstairs to get more iced tea for Grandma and suddenly he had Dad squawking at him all the way from New Zealand. Twig and Jas wandered in, and we all tried to listen but Zoran could only get a few words in here and there so the conversation didn't make much sense.

'I have spoken to Dr Reynolds . . .' 'Of course not a long-term solution . . .' 'Good well we shall see you soon . . .'

'What did he say?' I asked when he finally hung up.

'He's worried,' Zoran explained.

'He's cross,' I corrected. 'What did he *say*? What did you mean, long-term solution? Is Dad coming home?'

Zoran rubbed his face.

'He wants you all to go back to London,' he said. 'Cassie will meet you there. He needs a bit of time to sort out flights and square everything with his producer, then he'll come straight here and relieve me.'

'But we can't go home!' I said. 'I'm meant to be looking after Elsie!'

'I know,' Zoran said. 'And I haven't finished my sonata.'

Jas said, 'I don't know how my poem ends yet either.'

'Twig?' I asked, and he shrugged and said had anyone *seen* how many almost ripe tomatoes there were needing to be picked.

'So it's settled then,' I said. 'We're none of us leaving.'

Flora is back online. 'What did you say to make Dad so cross?' I asked her this evening.

'Only what you told me. I'm sorry it took so long to find him. I didn't realise he'd be moving around so much.'

'I think he doesn't really need to come after all. Grandma is much better.'

'Oh that's just marvellous,' Flora replied. 'After everything I've done!'

'None of us want to leave,' I explained.

'Does this have anything to do with those boys?'

'Maybe a little bit,' I admitted.

'Fine,' Flora wrote. 'I'll see what I can do.'

I love Flora, I really, really do.

Friday 15 August

After three days of bed and Zoran's cooking, Grandma is much better. Today she insisted on coming downstairs and going outside. At first Zoran wouldn't let her, so in the end they reached a compromise and we all helped carry a bed out to the garden where she lay like a queen all day, issuing orders – to Jas about her posture when she rode first Marigold and then Hester through the potager and into the walled garden. To Twig and me about how to tie tomato plants and deadhead roses. To Zoran about everything from how he shouldn't park the Land Rover in the sun to the best way to make pastry for his roasted vegetable tart.

'You are a bossy old woman,' he told her after lunch. 'But it is becoming clear to me that you are also much, much better. Perhaps the children were right to kidnap you after all.'

Grandma licked the last traces of his perfect gooseberry fool from her fingers, pronounced it too sour, and agreed that she was no good at being an invalid.

She cooked supper this evening, or rather she sat in the kitchen in an armchair Zoran brought in, throwing out comments like 'The sauce needs more oregano' and 'Those egg whites need to be standing to attention if your meringues are not going to disintegrate completely'.

'I have been cooking spaghetti on my own for *years*,' Jas informed her when Grandma said the pasta wasn't cooked.

'It doesn't mean you're good at it,' Grandma said.

Grandma decided tonight should be a feast, and

it really was. In the end, the pasta was perfect, and the sauce had just the right amount of oregano, the meringues were glossy and crisp on the outside and chewy and soft on the inside, the strawberries were delicious. After dinner, Twig did one of his favourite things when we are at Grandma's and played her old records on her turntable. Grandma lay with her feet up on the sofa, trying to teach us moves to dances like the jitterbug and the lindy hop, laughing her head off when we got it wrong and scoffing chocolates so fast you would never believe this was the woman who a few days ago thought her long dead dog had come to visit her in hospital.

I tried to sing along to the records and join in the dancing, but I couldn't concentrate because the boys come back tomorrow and I kept thinking, what if they come back early? All evening I was listening out for the sound of a car engine coming down the drive, or the squeak of unoiled bicycle wheels. At one point Elsie suddenly looked up and pricked her ears, and my heart nearly stopped.

Which was completely stupid. They're just boys. Not actors or rock stars. Boys, like Jake and Colin and Tom and a hundred others at school.

But different, all the same.

It's very different talking to someone on email and seeing them face to face.

I was so cool this morning. If Flora had been here, she would have been proud of me. Even though when I went to bed last night I was so jumpy I didn't know how I was going to stay alive till morning, when I woke up I made sure I did everything exactly how I always do, just to make sure nobody guessed how hard I was listening out for that car engine or those bike wheels. I read in bed for a bit (the same page over and over again, just like Twig and *Les Misérables*, which I think he's given up on), and then I got dressed really slowly in my most ordinary clothes and did my hair in plaits. They finally came (all of them, in the car) as we were having breakfast. Elsie hurled herself out of the back door squealing like a piglet with Jas and Twig not far behind, and I JUST CARRIED ON EATING MY CEREAL.

By the time I went out, Skye was already with the ponies, with Jas skipping about telling him how well she'd looked after Marigold and Hester, and Twig trying to interrupt her, and Elsie running joyful laps around the paddock, and I stopped worrying about what people would think and ran over to join them.

'Blue!' Ollie was sitting on the fence in his usual place, waving at me.

I think he's grown since he's been away. His pale gold skin is really brown so his eyes look really blue and his hair is bleached almost white.

He smiled. Nothing else mattered.

'Did you have a nice time?' I asked.

He was fumbling for something in his pocket. 'I got you something.'

'For me?'

'Ta da!'

He pulled out a little pale blue drawstring pouch and held it out towards me.

'What is it?'

'Open it!'

I loosened the drawstring and tipped the pouch over my palm. A delicate silver chain poured out, with a pendant shaped like a flower.

'It's a daisy,' Ollie said. 'I bought it at a market. I wanted to find you a bluebell, but they didn't have any.'

'It's so pretty.'

'Try it on,' Ollie said.

Skye and Jas were coming out of the paddock now,

with Elsie trotting at his heels being a meek and perfect dog. Skye turned to close the gate behind him, just as Ollie reached out to clasp the necklace round my neck.

Even from where I was standing, I saw his face freeze.

I raised my hand to wave, but Skye was already walking away.

Back in the kitchen, the grown-ups were arguing.

'Ah, Blue!' Lizzie cried as I came back in. 'Talk some sense into your lovely grandmother! I am offering to take you all to the beach tomorrow, but she won't hear of it.'

'I can take the children myself,' Grandma insisted.

'Constance, you really can't,' Zoran said. 'Let Lizzie take them in the Land Rover. I'll stay here with you.'

Jas and Twig came in, followed by Skye and Ollie.

'What's going on?' Twig asked.

Grandma raised her chin and she had that glint in her eye, the one that means she's not going to back down.

'I am taking you to the beach,' she said.

Lizzie and Zoran both started to protest, but no

one was paying attention to either of them, because Jas was jumping up and down and squealing. After Pumpkin, the ponies, Skye, Elsie, Gloria and writing poetry, the beach is her favourite thing.

'Finally!' she cried. 'Can we stay all day until the sun goes down? Can we have ice creams and eat them in the sea? Can we take nets and catch shrimps in rock pools and build a barbecue and cook them?'

'Madness!' cried Lizzie.

'Can we bury Zoran in the sand until only his head sticks out and plant a cross on him and pretend he's dead?'

'Certainly not,' said Zoran, but he had to turn away so we couldn't see his mouth twitch.

'Can we take Elsie and teach her to surf?'

Even Skye started to laugh.

'Well, Blue dear, it appears this whole outing depends on you.' Grandma's chin was still raised, but as she lifted her mug to her mouth I saw that her hands were shaking, and I thought how unfair it was of Lizzie to use words like *madness* talking about Grandma, and for Grandma not to be able to do the things she loves, and also for making me decide.

I met Skye's eye across the kitchen.

'I would love to go to the beach with you all tomorrow,' I said. Skye dropped his gaze and started scuffing the floor with his sneaker, but I could see that he was trying to hide a smile. I turned my head and saw Ollie watching us.

'Then it's decided!' Grandma crowed, and I turned back to her. I tried to speak as softly as possible.

'But Grandma, you really can't come. You know you can't. It's too hot, and you're only just getting better.'

The kitchen went very quiet. Twig and Jas shuffled closer to each other. Lizzie started to search through her bag for her car keys. Zoran cleared away the last breakfast things.

'I'll film it,' I said. 'Every single moment, so you'll feel like you were there.'

'But I won't be there, will I?' Grandma said. 'That's the point. I won't be there.'

She left. Ollie let out a long low whistle.

'It's not funny,' Skye said.

'I'm not laughing,' Ollie said.

Skye walked out.

I gathered Elsie's food and bowls and basket. Twig and Jas helped me carry them out to where Skye was leaning against his mum's car, chewing his thumbnail.

'I'm giving you Grandma's cardigan,' I said. 'I don't think she can ever wear it again.'

'Thanks,' he said.

'She was great. You know, after the pining. She really loves Grandma.'

'Everyone loves your Grandma.'

'My wish came true, you know. She's out of hospital.'

A smile flashed across his face. 'I told you it would,' he said.

'You said you bet it would,' I corrected.

'What wish?' asked Twig.

'At Melisandra's pool,' I said.

'You swam at Melisandra's pool?'

'Dude, you're the only one left who hasn't.' Ollie had come out too now. 'You have some serious catching up to do. Still scared of the dark?'

I realised then how much Twig's grown this summer. Not physically so much, but in other ways. He's gone from a kid who tried to impress people by reading a big book to a boy who rescues grandmothers from hospitals, a barefoot gardener who braves armies of bats. But I'd forgotten that side of Ollie, the side that can be a bit mean. Twig squirmed, and just like that he was a little kid again.

'What's it to you?' he said, but his voice was very tiny.

'Hey, Twig,' Skye said. 'At the beach. Want to learn to surf?'

'Sure.' Twig shrugged like it was no big deal, but he stopped squirming.

I smiled at Skye. He smiled back. Ollie stepped forward and draped his arm round my shoulders.

'Do you like Blue's necklace?' he asked.

Skye's gaze dropped to my throat. Ollie's arm tightened around my shoulder, like he knew I was trying to step away, and I wish my tummy wouldn't do that thing when he's near me.

It makes things so complicated.

I thought Skye would leave again, like he usually does when he doesn't like something. But he didn't, not immediately. Instead he looked at me, straight into my eyes like he never has before, and for once he didn't fumble or blush or do anything awkward, but said very softly so I almost couldn't hear, 'It doesn't matter if I like it or not. The question is, does Blue?'

And then he did leave. And Ollie left after him. And I have no idea what I think about anything.

Jas didn't even mind that Skye left before she could show off how much her riding has improved. She spent the day wandering around composing out loud, silly lines like 'Going to the beach, feeling like a peach', and singing 'Oh we do like to be beside the seaside'.

'Let her,' Grandma said when we tried to shut her up. 'It's nice that someone's happy.'

Grandma said Zoran should come to the beach with us too. Zoran said he didn't want to leave her alone, but she sighed that she was going to have to get used to it sooner or later and he couldn't stay with her forever, and even his plum tart with caramelised crème pâtissière didn't cheer her up.

The Film Diaries of Bluebell Gadsby

Scene Fourteen
A Day at the Beach!
(montage – to 'Octopus's
Garden', by the Beatles;
or 'By the Beautiful Sea',
by Harold Atteridge and
Harry Carroll; or any
other seaside song)

#1. Under a striped blue and white parasol, LIZZIE lies stretched out on a blanket, snoring gently, an upside down paperback covering her face, while ELSIE laps at the melted remains of an ice cream in the tub by her side.

#2. ZORAN rises like the living dead from his sand-grave and runs like a sand-monster, waving his arms and roaring, chasing a screaming JASMINE and TWIG into the sea.

#3. SKYE and Twig stand in the shallows, heads together, bent over a surfboard. Skye explains, Twig nods. Twig paddles out, catches a wave (this bit is easy, he's used to body surfing), tries to stand, falls backwards into the water. Tries again, and again, and again until the triumphant moment when he GETS it and surfs coolly in to shore, the sort of grin on his face once seen on a boy attempting to ride standing up on a cantering horse.

Everybody cheers.

#4 Elsie (crazy with ice cream?) knocks Twig off the board. He picks her up and puts her on in his place. Flat as a pancake, ears back, and growling, she crouches there as Skye, Jasmine and Twig paddle her through the shallows.

#5. OLLIE drags BLUEBELL into the waves. Together they dive again and again under the breakers crashing against the shore. He teases her, making her squeal as he pulls at her legs under the water. He tells her she looks like a mermaid (Ollie asks Lizzie to film this bit, though of course from that distance Lizzie can't pick up the sound and the mermaid comments are strictly private). She doesn't know how to respond.

#6. Lunch comes out, a bit sweaty. Curling sandwiches, oily cheese, crumbling cake, squashed bananas and warm ginger beer - they all go in seconds. People even ask for more.

The tide goes out. In the mellow light of late afternoon, Jasmine and Zoran search rock pools for shrimps. Ollie and Twig practise surfing, though there are hardly any waves (Ollie is the better surfer, of course). Now that the sea is calmer, Lizzie swims, a steady breaststroke. Skye comforts a fretting Elsie, who hates to see Lizzie in the water.

Picture sways as CAMERAMAN (BLUE) walks the length of the beach to the rocks at the end of the bay. She hangs the camera around her neck as she begins to climb. It catches a bare foot here, a hand, a knee, grey rock and gleaming pools, the dark red of a sea anemone, the flash of a shrimp, the white crenellated shell of a limpet. Cameraman sits and picture settles. She has found the most isolated spot on the beach, a wide rock ledge above the bay, an excellent vantage point, higher even than the cawing gulls. The view from here is all sky and sea, sunlight dancing on water, golden sand crowded with parasols, towels and people.

A figure detaches itself from the cheerful throng, walking towards the rocks.

Sandy hair. Broken glasses. Trips as he tries to avoid a small child with a bucket and spade.

The figure starts to climb. The figure is Skye.

'I got something for you too,' Skye mumbled. 'It's not as nice as Ollie's, I mean it's not silver or valuable or anything but I thought, you know. You might like it.'

Skye's present wasn't wrapped in a velvet pouch like Ollie's. It was in his shorts' pocket, and it was a little bit damp and a little bit sandy too. It was another pendant, a tiny iris this time, painted on a white ceramic disc on a short leather thong.

I got a lump in my throat.

'This guy was taking requests. I asked him to do this specially.'

'I love it,' I said.

Skye's face broke into the biggest smile.

'I thought the iris . . .'

'I'm going to wear it right now.'

I raised it to my throat. My fingers caught on Ollie's daisy.

'Oh,' I said.

'It doesn't matter,' Skye said. 'Just wear it whenever.'

'Let me just take this one off.'

'No, really. I just wanted you to have it. Keep the daisy on, it's pretty.'

He was already starting to scramble down the rocks.

'Skye, wait!' I shouted after him.

He stopped. 'I really do love it,' I said.

I thought he was going to say something, but then he just shook his head and dropped down to the beach.

I went after him, but by the time I caught up with him he was already with Lizzie. She was on the phone.

'Time to go,' she said, covering up the mouthpiece.

The others drifted back from the sea, and our day at the beach was over.

I played with both my necklaces all the way home, the one around my neck and the one in my pocket, the daisy that wasn't a bluebell and the iris, while Twig watched my video of him surfing over and over again, and Jas pelted me with questions about Melisandra's pool, like when did I go and did the water change colour and did my wish come true.

'It did,' I said and she said good, then hers would too.

It was night by the time we reached home but not dark, because the sky was clear and full of stars. Lizzie tooted the Citroën's horn as we approached the Horsehill turning, and waved goodbye. Zoran tooted back, and then we were driving down the lane and into the courtyard. We'd all been asleep, and it felt weird as we stumbled out of the car yawning and rubbing our eyes. Almost like a different kind of day had started.

'There's another car,' I noticed, and then the front door opened and Dad appeared.

'DADDY!' Jas shrieked and started running towards him.

'But Flora was meant to keep him in New Zealand!' I said.

'That is no way to react to your father's return,' Zoran scolded.

'I'm going to tell him about my surfing!' Twig said.

He sprinted after Jas. 'Hop it,' Zoran said, and I ran after Twig.

For a few moments, before he got cross, Dad was pleased. We used to climb over him all the time when we were little, but he's not so used to people hugging him any more. He gathered the three of us in his arms and it was like we were all tiny again. Nobody said anything except for 'Blue! Twig! Jas! Daddy!' and also 'I surfed, I surfed, I surfed!'

Grandma appeared on the front doorstep. 'Isn't this a lovely surprise?' she said.

'When did you get here?' I asked.

'This morning, just after you'd left for the beach,' Dad replied.

'Is Mum here too? What about Pumpkin?' Jas demanded.

'How was the beach?' Grandma questioned.

'I surfed!'

'Where's Flora?' I asked.

'Come in, come in!' Dad cried. 'Don't keep your grandmother waiting on the doorstep.'

Everything's different with Dad here. I mean, I love him, but he's different from Zoran. The way he insists on doing things for Grandma, it's not like he's trying to help. It's more like he's trying to take over.

'Let's make hot chocolate,' Grandma said as we went in.

'I'll do it,' Dad said.

'I am perfectly capable of making hot chocolate for my grandchildren,' Grandma sighed.

'But I *want* to do it.'

Grandma tugged the pan away from Dad, slammed it on the kitchen range, poured in a big carton of milk and started bashing a bar of chocolate on the kitchen counter.

Dad tried to take her arm. 'You need to rest,' he said.

'I have been resting all day,' Grandma declared, still bashing.

'But I came back to look after you!' Dad cried.

'Blue's got a video. Show him, Blue.'

'For God's sake, Twig!' Dad shouted. 'Now is not the time to talk about your bloody surfing!'

'Well there was absolutely no need.' Grandma dropped the smashed chocolate into the pan, splashing milk all over herself. 'As you can see, there is nothing wrong with me at all.'

Jas, who had been very quiet, asked why Mum and Pumpkin weren't here, and would they be coming soon. Dad said he didn't know but they both needed peace and quiet and there was obviously little chance of that here. Jas started to cry that she would never be happy again and ran outside. Grandma announced that she was going upstairs to run herself a bath and that Zoran should take over making the hot chocolate. Zoran was in the scullery, shovelling beach towels into the washing machine, and didn't hear. The chocolate boiled over and burned.

'I WAS WORRIED ABOUT YOU!' Dad yelled up the stairs to Grandma.

Jas came back in from the garden and announced that Twig had gone, and so had his bike.

'What do you mean, gone?' Dad asked.

'I can't find him.'

'He probably went to bed, to get away from all the commotion.' Zoran looked disapprovingly at Dad when he said 'commotion', but Dad pretended not to notice and started to go upstairs, saying it was high time Jas went to bed too.

'His *bike* has gone,' Jas protested. 'He wouldn't take his bike to *bed*.'

'He must have left it somewhere,' Zoran said.

Jas stamped her foot and said Twig always leaves his bike in exactly the same place, which is true – right by the edge of the drive, next to where Dad's car is parked, facing the road so if there's an emergency, he says, he can make a quick getaway.

'I'll go and check,' I told her.

The bike wasn't in its usual place. I looked everywhere else, including the paddock and the potager, but I couldn't find it.

'He's not in his room.' Dad was coming downstairs as I went back into the house.

'I *told* you,' Jas said.

'Or anywhere downstairs.' Zoran came out of the scullery, looking worried. 'Unless he's hiding.'

'Why would he hide?' Dad cried.

'I imagine he's gone for a nice moonlit ride, to get some peace and quiet.' Grandma was back downstairs now too, in her dressing gown, ready for her bath.

'It's not that,' Jas said, but no one was listening to her.

'A nice moonlit ride?' Dad was frantic now. 'Without telling anyone? He's twelve years old, for heaven's sake! Does he have lights? Is he wearing a helmet? You make it sound so normal!'

Grandma said she thought riding a bicycle in the moonlight would be a lovely thing to do, but if Dad was so worried they should go out searching for him.

'You drive towards Plumpton,' she said. 'And I will go over the moor. We'll easily catch up with him.'

'You are not driving anywhere!' Dad yelled. 'You've been ill, you can't go tearing around the countryside in the middle of the night.'

'Often we cycle on paths,' I told him.

He looked at me blankly.

'Across the moors,' I clarified.

'Is anybody going to listen to me?' Jas complained.

Dad cried, 'Oh my God the marshes!' and ran out of the room.

'The marshes?' Zoran asked.

'People drown in them,' I explained. 'They're all over the moor.'

'Oh, sweet Lord!' Zoran said, and he ran out after Dad.

Grandma was a bit bewildered by Dad's behaviour.

'Where does he think he's going?' she asked.

'It's his fault,' Jas said. 'Twig did try to tell him about surfing.'

Grandma looked even more bewildered. 'But where has he gone?'

'To Satan's Tor, of course,' Jas said. 'To prove that he is worthy.'

'To get Dad's attention,' I said. I thought of Ollie and Melisandra, Twig squirming, Twig looking small. 'And to prove he isn't afraid. Of course! I have to get Skye.'

'Why?' Grandma asked.

'No one knows Satan's Tor better than him.'

'Oh, no you don't!' Grandma grabbed me as I was running out to my bike, and marched me back into the house. 'You can use the telephone like a normal person,' she said. 'I'm not having two children gallivanting about the countryside on bicycles, however lovely the moon.'

Gallivanting. I swear that's what she said.

Skye answered the phone. I told him what had

happened. A few minutes later, he came flying down the drive on his bike and skidded to a halt.

'Get your bike, Blue, and we'll go after him!' he cried.

'I'm coming too!' Jas cried.

'You have all lost your minds,' Grandma declared. 'If Twig is cycling to Satan's Tor, you'll never catch up with him on bikes.' She pulled her dressing gown tighter around her, kicked off her slippers and rammed her feet into her purple Crocs. 'We'll go after him in the car!'

'Are you sure?' I said. 'I don't think you're supposed to drive.'

'Where's Ollie?' Jas asked Skye.

'He couldn't come.'

We climbed into the Land Rover, me and Jas in the back, Skye in the front next to Grandma. She drove hunched over the wheel, like somehow that would make it easier to see Twig. We were all quiet, peering out of the windows. It was scary, up on the moor at night. Different from riding out with Skye. The darkness then was an adventure, but tonight it just felt ... big. Up there on the open road, even the stars which had shone so brightly in the garden seemed paler.

None of us saw Twig until it was too late. We had

expected him to be on a bike, up ahead of us, but he burst out of the darkness on foot, straight into the path of the Land Rover.

And Zoran's right. It does pull to the left.

'He came out of nowhere!' Grandma kept saying afterwards, and also, 'A split second before there was nobody there!'

Twig's pale face loomed out of the night like a Dartmoor ghost, and everybody screamed. Even Skye. Even Grandma.

I have to get this right. Dad says he wants to know exactly what happened.

Twig appeared and Grandma screamed and the steering wheel pulled to the left and Grandma drove off the road.

Grandma drove off the road and Twig leapt out of her way and fell to the ground. Grandma skidded into a ditch and crashed into a rock. There was the sound of glass smashing. Metal buckling. A lot of people screaming. Jas flew off her seat into me and we both fell to the floor of the Land Rover, except it wasn't really the floor any more – we were squashed up under my seat, on what should have been the side.

And then no one moved. Jas started to cry.

'Grandma?' I whispered. 'Grandma, are you all right?'

She moaned, and I almost started crying myself.

'Skye?'

'OK,' he croaked. His face appeared on the other side of the dog guard.

'Can you see Twig?'

'No. Can you get out?'

The car lurched a bit as I inched towards the back door. Jas whimpered and clutched my arm. I squeezed her and whispered to her to let me go, then moved again. This time the car stayed still, even when I pulled on the handle and kicked the door.

The warm night air rushed in. I stopped to breathe it then reached back for Jas.

'Slowly,' I said.

She crawled out after me and then we were both outside, and Twig was sitting rolled up in a ball by the side of the road on Grandma's side of the car, not even crying but shaking as he stared at the Land Rover.

'You're all right!'

'I got a puncture,' he whispered. 'So I walked. But now my ankle hurts.'

There was a creak of metal behind us. We turned to look. Skye was climbing out of the upturned passenger door, very careful not to make any sudden moves. He slid down to the ground and staggered over to us.

'We have to get your Grandma out. She's conscious, and she can move all her limbs, but she's cut her head and I think she's in shock.'

The Land Rover shifted again when we clambered over the passenger side to get to the door.

'Wait for the grown-ups,' Jas cried.

'What if it catches fire?' Twig worried.

'That only happens in films,' I said. 'And what grown-ups? Dad and Zoran are running about on the moor, and I'm just as strong as Lizzie.'

'But they'll know what to do!'

'They never know what to do,' I said.

'Shut up and help me,' Skye said.

In the end, Grandma got out by wrapping her arms round Skye's neck. He pulled her up onto the edge of the doorframe. Jas held the door open so it wouldn't slam on them. I helped Grandma to slide down and took her to sit on a rock, where she told me that she was perfectly fine then burst into tears at the sight of Twig, limping towards her but otherwise unharmed.

'We need to go back and get a car for them.' I've never seen Skye like he was tonight, other than when he's riding. He didn't stumble or trip once. 'Twig, I'll take your bike.'

'It's got a puncture,' Jas told him.

Skye swore and asked, did Twig have a puncture repair kit? Twig said he didn't, and Skye swore some more.

'I guess I'll have to run,' Skye said. 'I'm probably the fastest.'

He looked dubiously down the long dark road.

'I'll go with you,' I offered.

'You'll slow me down.'

'I'm a good runner!' I know that was a lie, but it was so obvious Skye didn't want to go alone. I'm not the only one who thought the moor looked spooky. Jas announced that she was coming too.

'You really will slow us down,' I told her.

'If anything attacks us,' Jas said, 'I would rather be with you.'

Grandma stopped crying and started to laugh a bit hysterically. Twig went even paler and said, 'Maybe we should all go.'

'With that foot?' I said.

'I could hop.'

'We'll be back as quick as we can.' Skye was pulling blankets and cushions out of the back of the Land Rover, and I put them round Grandma. 'Are you warming up?' I asked.

'I feel such a fool.'

'It's not your fault, it's Twig's.' Twig looked indignant. I frowned at him. 'Anyway, no one's hurt.' Twig looked even more outraged. His ankle was already swelling up and there was blood on Grandma's face. 'Not badly, anyway,' I said.

'You ought to eat something,' Skye said. 'Is there anything in the car? Sweets or something?'

Twig reached into his rucksack and produced a family-size bar of milk chocolate.

'I thought I might need it,' he said without meeting our eyes.

Skye crouched down in front of Twig. His glasses were all crooked again, but somehow he still managed to look very serious.

'I know it's dark,' he said. 'But you need to look after your Grandma. We'll be back as soon as we can with a car to take you back.'

Twig nodded. I've never seen him look so brave.

Dad was pacing up and down outside the house when we got back. Zoran was doing that thing he does with his hands when he's trying to calm us, like he's saying slow down. Dad was doing that thing *he* does when he's in a state, which is throw his hands up in the air and wave them.

'We found him!' Jas shouted as we ran up to them. 'He's on Satan's Tor with Grandma!'

'What?' I noticed his hands didn't quite stop waving. 'How? Where? Why?'

'He got a puncture,' Skye explained. 'And Mrs Gadsby crashed the Land Rover.'

'They're all right,' I added. 'But they need you to go and fetch them.'

'Why, why, why can my family never be normal?' Dad's waving was frantic again as he marched towards his car.

'Shall I go with him?' Skye murmured.

'That would probably be best,' I whispered back.

'Questions later,' Zoran said, after they'd gone. 'Strong, sweet tea now, I think. Also, brandy. And probably toast.'

When he's not actively panicking, Zoran can be stupendous in a crisis. I'm glad it was him with us when we went back in, and not Dad. I don't think Dad could have coped. Not after flying from New Zealand, and driving from London, arguing with Grandma, Twig disappearing and then the crash. Today was like a day that never ends, and it was almost too much even for us.

We went back in through the front door.

'What's that noise?' Jas asked as we walked down the passage towards the kitchen.

'It sounds like someone left the tap running,' Zoran said, pushing open the door.

Someone *had* left a tap running. Two taps, to be precise. Grandma's bathroom is right above the kitchen, and by the time we got home the water from her bath was pouring through the ceiling.

The Film Diaries of Bluebell Gadsby

Scene Fifteen
What Happened at Breakfast

DAYTIME. INTERIOR.

The kitchen at Horsehill Farm. JASMINE,
ZORAN, TWIG and FATHER sit at the table,
eating breakfast (toast and cereal –
Jasmine wanted sausages but Father said
no). Zoran and Father look haggard (they
have not slept all night). Buckets,
basins, saucepans and salad bowls are
stacked on the floor. From the scullery
next door comes the sound of the
washing machine, running yet another
load of towels, dishcloths and assorted
rags used to mop up last night's flood.
Through the open window, the first two
loads can be seen fluttering on the
washing-line. The ceiling above the

table is one big dark grey patch of
damp, yellow at the edges. A long crack
runs through it, from which every few
seconds a fat brown drop of water plops
into a pan strategically placed between
the fruit bowl and the marmalade.

ZORAN
(trying to be optimistic)
At least it's only a little drip.

TWIG
The crack has got bigger.

FATHER
I don't think it's got bigger.

JASMINE
Why can't I have sausages?

FATHER
Because Zoran and I have spent the
last twelve hours cleaning up mess
and we can't face more washing up.
Also, I am severely jet-lagged. No
one seems at all aware of this fact.

                    JASMINE
          We all helped. I can cook them
            myself. I would also do the
                   washing up.

                CAMERAMAN (Bluebell)
          The last time you cooked sausages,
          you nearly set fire to the kitchen.

Father groans and clutches his head.

                     ZORAN
            You're right, Twig, it *is*
                 getting bigger.

                      TWIG
            It's sort of *bowing*.

Father looks up impatiently. His
expression changes as he realises
that the ceiling is indeed bowing,
and that over the course of breakfast
the crack has grown considerably
larger. He pushes his chair back,
gesturing to others to do the same.
They exchange questioning glances but

obey. They stand back from the table (Twig on one leg, because of his foot) but nobody speaks, as if they are afraid that the slightest noise would invoke disaster.

And yet disaster happens.

First there is a loud CREAK, and then the ceiling collapses. Fragments of plaster, bits of board, pieces of wood and a tonne of sand crash and shower down. Clouds of thick grey dust explode and rise up. Breakfast is obliterated.

All stare, awestruck.

FATHER
Bloody hell.

JASMINE (in a very small voice)
Is it over?

More creaking, this time louder and more sustained. All look up. Grandma's claw-footed, cast-iron bathtub sails through the air and lands with a shattering thud on the kitchen table.

The table buckles and collapses. There
is a lot more dust.

ZORAN
(peering up through hole in ceiling)
Now I think it's over.

Grandma ordered me to film breakfast. 'You are my eyes and ears,' she told me when I went in with her cup of tea this morning. 'I want to know everything your father says about me.'

Dad didn't say much about Grandma at all during breakfast, owing to the ceiling and the jet lag and before that the towels and pans and mops and things, but he had plenty to say to her afterwards.

The first thing Dad did last night after he got home with the others was call Dr Reynolds. Dr Reynolds doesn't normally do home visits at night, but when Dad explained about the accident and how Twig's ankle was swollen like a tennis ball and Grandma had hit her head, he said he would come right over.

Dr Reynolds confirmed that Twig's ankle isn't broken, just twisted. I think Twig was a bit disappointed at first, until Dr Reynolds told him that a bad twist is often worse than a clean break.

'We'll have to get you some crutches,' he said, and Twig brightened up a lot.

Dr Reynolds was much more worried about Grandma.

Jas and I took a break from mopping to sneak up

to her room. We stood outside her half-open door. She was sitting up in bed drinking Zoran's hot sweet tea and brandy with a packet of frozen peas round her neck.

'She looks like a proper ghost,' Jas said.

'Don't say that.'

'Why?'

'If she was a proper ghost, she'd be dead.'

Grandma looked tired and sad and frightened. Dr Reynolds said she has mild whiplash (hence the frozen peas) and possibly concussion, and that somebody should stay with her overnight to check on her once every hour.

'I'll do it,' I said.

Dr Reynolds jumped. 'Where did you come from?' he asked.

Zoran said that we spend half our lives listening at doors, and that he would look after Grandma because it was a job for grown-ups.

'I'm fourteen,' I told him.

'Exactly,' he said.

Dr Reynolds stayed to have a drink with Dad after he'd seen Grandma, while Jas and I carried on mopping.

'I need a whisky,' I heard Dad say.

'And I need to talk to you,' Dr Reynolds replied.

They sat together in the two leather chairs in front of the living-room fireplace, and they talked for ages. After Dr Reynolds had gone, Dad came into the kitchen and I thought he was going to cry. At the time, I thought it was because of the state of the place, which really would have been perfectly understandable. Water was still pouring through the ceiling. Jas and I had moved the table, and the floor was like a giant patchwork of pots and pans and buckets, with multi-coloured towels all around and underneath them to catch the splashes. In a way, it was pretty, and I sort of wish I'd filmed it. But only in a way. And only sort of.

'I'll take over,' Dad said. 'You girls go to bed.'

'We want to help.'

'Please just do as I say.'

He followed us up the stairs.

'Jas, you sleep with your sister tonight,' he said.

'I want to look after Twig.'

'Don't argue.'

Dad saw us to my bedroom door, then went in to Twig. I paused to listen on my way back from the bathroom.

'Why?' I heard him ask.

Twig mumbled something that sounded like 'Grandpa's story.'

'*Grandpa's*?'

'The legend of Satan's Tor.' Dr Reynolds gave Twig some very strong painkillers. It sounded like he was already asleep. 'Staying out all night.'

'But what were you thinking?'

'I wanted' – yawn, yawn – 'you to be proud.'

'Proud! What are you talking about? Twig, you are my only son!'

I stuck my head around the door. 'Actually,' I objected, 'he's not.'

'Go away!' Dad commanded. 'Twig, you are my only *eldest* son! I will always love you, *always*. Nothing can ever change that.'

I peeped round the edge of the door. Dad glared at me. Twig was sleeping, cradled in Dad's arms, and he was smiling.

This morning, after the bath came through the ceiling and Dad had made sure nobody was hurt, he went up to see Grandma for a really, really long time. And now I know why he looked so upset last night.

'People could have been killed!' we heard him say, and also, 'You are a danger to yourself and others!'

'And you have a gift for melodrama!' Grandma retorted, but her voice was shaky.

Zoran came up and made us go back downstairs.

He said that today was no time to be listening at doors.

'Is she sick?' I questioned.

'Be patient,' Zoran said.

'We're not very good at that,' Jas told him.

Then the surgery rang and said they had Twig's crutches, and the others all drove off to Plumpton to get them. I was alone in the kitchen picking up towels when Dad finally came down.

'Look at this place,' he said.

'I'm trying to tidy it,' I told him.

'Well don't,' he sighed. 'Not until I've called a builder to make sure it's safe. God, and a plumber too. And someone to tow the Land Rover.'

He slumped down on a chair in the hall. 'Could you get me the phone book?'

I brought him the Yellow Pages. I helped him find a builder and an emergency plumber in Plumpton, then I sat next to him on the floor while he made his phone calls.

'What's happening to Grandma?' I asked when he'd finished.

'It's nothing for you to worry about.'

'But I am worried.'

Dad ran his hands through his hair again. It was full of dust and plaster. Mine was too. Everything is.

'Things keep happening,' he sighed. 'But she won't see it, and every time they leave her a little bit weaker. She forgets things, she has trouble walking...'

'No she doesn't!' I said. 'I went for a walk with her and she went so fast I couldn't keep up!'

'Well she shouldn't,' Dad said. 'She has dizzy spells. She pushes herself too hard and then she exhausts herself.'

'Grandma's amazing,' I said. 'Just ask Lizzie. She's always saying so.'

'Lizzie's worried too.'

I got cross then and said it wasn't fair to all gang up on Grandma. I reminded him of all the things Grandma does, like what an awesome cook she is, and how good she is at working in the garden, and how much fun we have with her.

'I'm not saying she isn't fun,' Dad said. 'But be honest, Blue – how much is she actually doing herself? Flora and I do talk, you know. She told me how much you've been helping, and I know how much Lizzie does, and her son. I have to do more and more basic things for her – her phone was cut off after her fall because she forgot to pay the bill. Same with the electricity.'

My mind went back to the first day of the holidays, waiting in the station car park at Plumpton.

Grandma screeching up an hour late, not even realising. The afternoon naps. Falling ill because she worked too hard. The way she sometimes walks fast and easily, but sometimes hobbles like her weight is too much to carry. And then I thought about the night before she went to hospital, and the horrible old people's ward, and my eyes stung.

Dad pulled me close.

'She's just getting old, love,' he said. 'That's all it is.'

'What's going to happen to her?' I asked.

Dad said, 'Well she can't stay here. Tom agrees. The house is much too big for one old lady. She's going to have to move.'

Mum's coming tomorrow. Twig spoke to her for ages this afternoon. His ankle is dark purple now, ringed with red and still swollen, but after he put the phone down I swear he looked so happy I thought that he would run and jump and skip. She's coming tomorrow.

'All our wishes are coming true,' Jas sighed, but here's the thing I'm learning with wishes, as soon as they come true, more queue up behind them.

Ollie has gone. Lizzie rang just after Mum. She was on her way to Plumpton, taking him to the station and wanted to know if we needed groceries, and that's how I found out. Zoran shouting to me from the phone in the hall while I was in the kitchen, asking could I check if we'd run out of dishwasher tablets and were we low on butter.

He didn't even say goodbye.

'Probably embarrassed,' Jas said darkly. 'Because of teasing Twig, and not coming out while everyone was out looking for him.'

'I'm sure there's a reason,' I said.

I went out for a very, very long walk. I don't even want to write about it.

The necklace. Those mermaid comments.

I thought he liked me at least a bit.

This evening Dad asked me not to mention any of what he told me about Grandma and the house to the others, because he didn't want to upset them. 'What about upsetting me?' I asked and he said it was different for me, because I am older.

The Film Diaries of Bluebell Gadsby

Scene Sixteen
Sunrise Again

EXTERIOR. DAWN.

In the little hollow at the top of
Satan's Tor, SKYE leans back against
the high outcrop of rock, eating
fruitcake. Elsie lies draped over
his feet, on the lookout for crumbs
as usual. In the half-light of early
morning, they look like shadows,
but the pale sky grows more blue
with every minute and soon the boy
and his dog, like the world around
them, will come into sharp colour.
The first rays of sun are piercing
through in the east, brushing the
undersides of clouds with hints of
pink and gold.

Skye pushes himself up to kneeling, brushing cake off his clothes. Elsie snuffles at the grass.

> SKYE
> (starts to crawl)
> I'm going to watch from the edge.

> CAMERAMAN (BLUEBELL)
> What? No! You'll fall.

> SKYE
> No I won't.

He crawls, or rather slithers, along the short spiky grass right to the edge of the cliff. Elsie whines. Just watching him CAMERAMAN almost drops the camera in an attack of vertigo. Skye lies flat on his front, then pushes himself onto his elbows, face resting in his hands. He turns his head and grins, then reaches out a hand. Cameraman inches backwards.

SKYE

(softly)

It's worth it, I promise.

Picture jumps about as Cameraman drags herself to the edge. She gives a startled squeak, but as picture straightens the whole world comes into view. Further back, the picture was mainly sky. From here, the lens fills with moors and heather and fields and woods and streams going on forever, miles beneath, and Cameraman gets that feeling again, that the world has just been born.

Cameraman starts to cry.

I woke up with a jump this morning, convinced that it was the middle of the night and that someone was in my room, and I was almost right. It was still dark outside, and a boy was climbing through my window.

For a wild moment, I thought that it was Ollie. Then I saw that it was Skye.

'How?' I asked when I could speak, and also, 'Why?'

'Ladder,' Skye replied. 'From the tree. And I thought, I mean I wondered, would you like to go for another ride?'

After I started crying, we slid backwards on our tummies to the rock, and sat in the grassy hollow. Skye put his arm around me, and I put my head on his shoulder.

'I told Ollie he couldn't just leave like that,' Skye said.

'It doesn't matter.'

'Yes it does. Look, he didn't want me to tell you this, I mean he doesn't want anyone to know, but I think it's just dumb. You know his parents, when they came here?'

I nodded. And then he told me the truth about everything.

How Ollie's parents did go to Italy, but it wasn't to celebrate their anniversary, it was a last attempt to save their marriage after Ollie's dad had an affair.

How it didn't work, and when they came down, it was to tell Ollie they were getting divorced.

How the day we went to the beach, the phone call Lizzie got when we were packing up was from Ollie's mother, saying his father was moving out.

'That's why he didn't come out looking for Twig,' Skye said. 'And why he left in such a hurry.'

'He was too upset,' I sighed. 'And he wanted to be with his mum. Oh, poor Ollie.'

Skye picked up a stone and started stabbing with it at the grass.

'What?' I asked. 'Don't you feel sorry for him?'

'Of course I do. I'd hate for my parents to split up. I just . . .'

He threw the stone over the edge of the cliff and picked up another one.

'*What*?'

'He didn't want anyone to know because he didn't want people to feel sorry for him. I get that. But it's not an excuse to hurt people.'

'He didn't hurt . . .'

'Yes he did. He made Twig feel small, and he lied to you. He made you think you were important to him, but actually what he wanted was for you to like him more than me. He didn't want anything to do with you at first. He used to make us come super-early in the morning, like way before I would normally wake up. His actual words were "Dude, that girl and those kids? No way." I'm sorry, I shouldn't be telling you this.'

'But afterwards.' My chest hurt and it was hard to speak. 'Afterwards, we became friends.'

'Sure. After he saw us talking, that time I fell of Marigold, he was all "Let's go to the river" and stuff. He hates that Mum and Dad are happy, and he didn't want . . .'

'What?'

'He didn't want me to be friends with you, even though he knew . . .'

He stopped, and threw the second stone over the edge.

'He knew you didn't have any friends,' I finished softly.

If that was true, it was unforgivable. And yet in my heart of hearts, I knew that I forgave him.

He picked up a third stone. I reached out and took it from him, and then because he looked so upset I held his hand, and it was his turn to put his head on my shoulder.

'It's just rubbish,' he said. 'I had loads of friends in France, and I had a job at the stables, and it was all cool. Then Mum decides I have to get English qualifications, even though I'm doing OK in French school, and Dad's all hey, let's live on Dartmoor for no reason other than he used to come here on holiday when he was a kid, and suddenly I'm in the middle of nowhere, and everyone at school's known each other since they were practically babies, and it's obvious I don't belong.'

'I think you belong,' I said. 'Not at school, maybe. But here. I've never seen anyone belong more.'

'It's better since you came.'

And then we sat there a bit longer, looking at the sky.

'My dad says we have to sell Horsehill,' I told him.

'I know. Mum told me. That's the other reason I came.'

I squeezed his hand harder. He squeezed back.

'Grown-ups *are* rubbish,' I said. 'Ollie's parents. Your parents. My parents. They do all these things, like split up and move countries and have babies and sell houses, and they just expect you to be OK with it.'

'You really like him, don't you? Even though he lied and didn't say goodbye.'

Even though he never messaged once when he went away, even though he *was* mean to Twig, even though he probably didn't care about me. I sighed. Skye's arm tightened around my shoulder.

'Why do we always like the wrong people?' I whispered.

'I don't know.'

'Skye, do you like me?'

'I love you.'

I craned my neck to look up at him.

'Not like that,' he said quickly. 'I thought I did, I mean I thought maybe I would. I do fall in love quite a lot, actually. But I haven't. Maybe because I like you too much. I don't know. Do you mind?'

I started to laugh.

I wanted to tell him I loved him too, but I didn't want it to sound like I was just saying it because he had.

'Look!' I reached under the neckline of my sweatshirt. 'I'm wearing your present.'

He smiled, but he looked a bit sad too.

'I love it,' I insisted.

'You love it because of the iris.'

And I felt a little bit guilty then. Because yes, I

do love it for the iris. But I love it also because Skye *thought* about the iris. And it was like that time walking on the moor with Elsie. I'm not sure if I like that, I'm not sure I'm ready for it, because if it's true, then does it mean he's taken a little bit of her place in my heart, like Pumpkin has in Mum's?

So I didn't tell him. Not at first, anyway. We sat there for a bit longer, and then we scrambled back down to the ponies. The sun was hot on the way home. I took my sweatshirt off and tied it around my waist.

The little iris pendant glinted. Skye glanced sideways at it. I put my hand up to touch it, and then I told him.

'Not just because of the iris,' I admitted.

Skye grinned wider than I've ever seen before.

The ponies trotted on, eager for home. It was only as we turned down the lane that it hit us. 'If they sell Horsehill,' Skye said, 'how will I see you again?'

Jas was waiting for us when we came back, sitting on the paddock fence. I thought she would be jealous, riding being her thing to do with Skye, but the minute she saw us she stood up and started to wave.

'Hurry!' she shouted. 'They've caught the early train!'

Jas's excitement was contagious. Everyone started to rush around getting ready to go to the station. Jas brushed her hair and replaced her dirty old dress with an almost clean one. Twig found his shoes and washed his face and hands. Grandma ordered Dad to pick some flowers and Zoran roused himself from his piano composition to announce he would make another plum tart for lunch.

I didn't go with them to the station. I could picture the scene. Jas slipping under the ticket barrier and running down the platform. Twig on crutches. Mum crying when she saw his foot. Pumpkin gurgling, or howling, or sleeping, and everyone cooing over him whatever he did.

'I'll help Zoran make the tart,' I said.

'But don't you want to see them *immediately*?' Jas asked.

'I'll see them when they get here. Really.'

The thing is, what I realised as they were all rushing about getting ready to go, is that I've hardly thought about Pumpkin for ages. And this morning, seeing Jas so excited, it brought it all back and I felt ... jealous. Not of him, but of them. Because however turbulent their own adjustment to Pumpkin has been in the past, today they make it look so easy.

'Cheer up,' Zoran said as I laid the table.

'You don't understand,' I told him.

I was in my room when they came back. I heard the car and looked out of the window. Mum stepped out first. She was wearing that dress I like, the purple one with the little yellow flowers, and yellow sneakers to match. Her hair was pulled back in a messy bun like the one I tried to do, except on her it *did* look elegant and sophisticated and not at all like a teacher or librarian. She opened the back door and started fussing over Pumpkin in his car seat, and then he was here too, with his shock of red hair and looking almost twice as big as when we left him in London. Zoran came out and kissed Mum. Jas held her arms out for Pumpkin.

'Look at his tooth!' she said to Zoran.

She slid her little finger into Pumpkin's mouth. He clamped it shut. She squealed, delighted.

'He bit me!'

Pumpkin released her finger. She held him up above her head. 'Naughty baby,' she cooed. He made a sort of gurgling noise, like he was laughing at her, and everyone else laughed too.

'Where's Blue?' Mum asked Zoran.

'Upstairs.'

Mum's like Iris. She never walks if she can run.

There was the sound of light quick footsteps up the stairs and along the landing, my bedroom door was thrown open, and there she was, looking quite breathless and a bit dishevelled. She slowed down though when she came into the room. She walked up to the window where I was still standing and stood in front of me.

'Look at my necklace,' I said.

She slipped a finger under it to lift it to the light. I raised my chin so she could see it better.

'Pretty,' she whispered.

And then she hugged me, a fierce, long, close hug.

I read somewhere once that the more you love a person, the more the heart keeps growing.

Maybe the heart grows the more people you love, too. Pumpkin hasn't replaced Iris for Mum any more than Skye has for me. People don't get replaced, not really. Just, new ones come along and fill some of the space the old ones left behind.

It's not the same thing at all.

Pumpkin smiled at me today. Mum laid out a rug in the shade in the garden. She took all his clothes off so he wouldn't be too hot and he loved it. He is so white he glows, and his skin has the same transparency as Grandma's, except his is taut and plump instead of wrinkled. He lay on his back on the blanket with his feet in his mouth, staring up at the leaves of an apple tree like he'd never seen anything so amazing in his life. I waited until nobody was looking, which is harder than it sounds. When it comes to Pumpkin, somebody is *always* looking. But there was a moment this afternoon, when Jas drifted away to talk to Marigold and Hester, and Twig set up the backgammon board with Zoran and Dad was indoors and Mum wanted tea, when she left me alone with him.

I sat down next to him. He ignored me. I rolled over so I was on all fours above him with my plaits hanging down, tickling his shoulders. He grabbed one of them and pulled. I said, 'Ow!' He chuckled. He pulled again. 'That hurts,' I told him. And that is when he did it. A huge smile, bigger even than Skye's, so big it was like he was nothing *but* smile.

Straight at me.

Wednesday 20 August

Dad called out to me from the study this morning as I came in from helping Skye with the ponies. He was staring at his laptop, and I couldn't help noticing how smart he looked. Not office-smart or anything, but not his usual scruffy 'I'm an artist' look either – clean, and shaved, and he'd ironed his shirt.

'Flora wants to talk to you,' he said, without looking up from the screen. 'She came back to London without telling anybody, and she has been calling every ten minutes since about half past eight. I didn't know she was capable of getting up so early. Please make her stop.'

'I suppose you've been out hurling yourself off bridges again,' Flora said as I picked up.

'Why aren't you in New Zealand?' I asked.

'They axed me. Not me, I mean my character. She wasn't supposed to die, but Henry – he's the director – was pissed off with me about the whole Brandon-Dad-whales thing. I had to bubble up blood, then I changed my flight and came straight home because Zach gets back from Ireland tomorrow, so I thought I'd surprise him. And please don't ask about Brandon. If you bothered to read the occasional magazine, you'd know he's totally in love with his boyfriend. I told you from the beginning, we're just friends. I'm sorry, by the way, I couldn't keep Dad in New Zealand. There was no way he would stay. It was like trying to hold back a bull in a china shop once it's decided to smash everything in sight.'

'This is all quite a lot to assimilate,' I said.

'The point,' Flora announced, 'is Gloria. I went to see her. She's emigrating to Argentina.'

'Argentina?'

'They have really good horses. She says she wants a whole new start. She says, if Zoran really loves her, he will go too.'

We still don't have a kitchen table. After talking to Flora, I took my cereal bowl out to the bench in the garden. Zoran came out while I was eating and sat on the bench beside me, clutching a mug of coffee and looking shocked.

'You've spoken to Gloria then,' I said.

He sighed, and gulped his coffee.

'You have to leave,' I said. 'Go to London! Tell her you can't live without her!'

'I have to finish my sonata,' Zoran said.

'You're so stubborn.'

'*Argentina*?'

'Zoran, it's *Gloria*!'

'You're too young to understand,' Zoran muttered, and dragged himself back towards the house. Soon the sound of his sonata drifted out of the open window again, except this morning it sounded like a really tragic funeral march.

Twig limped out with a jam sandwich.

'What's with Zoran's music?' he asked.

I told him. He said Argentina sounded brilliant.

'They'll split up forever if we don't stop her,' I said. 'And then Flora will blame me.'

'Here's Grandma,' Twig said.

Grandma was even more depressed than Zoran. She sat between us in her dressing gown with a shawl over her shoulders, looking even smaller than in her hospital bed, and refused to be helpful. 'Argentina is a wonderful country,' she said. 'Gloria should enjoy her life while she's still young.'

'But Zoran!' I cried.

'My sunhat has disappeared,' Grandma murmured. 'And my cashmere cardigan. Sometimes I think I'm losing my mind.'

'Should we tell her?' Twig asked, but Grandma was back on her feet already, shuffling back towards the house.

I sat on the bench for a long time after they had all gone, watching. Mum and Dad came out, got in the car and drove away. Jas went down to the paddock with Pumpkin to show him the ponies. Lizzie arrived with a box of eggs, and joined me on the bench.

'I have to go away for a couple of days to see my sister,' she said. 'Skye explained, didn't he? She can't be alone right now. Skye doesn't want to come. I know it's terrible timing, with Granny ill, but I wanted to ask your parents if he could stay here.'

'My parents are out,' I said. 'But I'm sure it will be fine. He can share with Twig. Jas can move in with me.'

Skye at Horsehill. It seems right, somehow.

'Send my love to Ollie,' I said, and I tried to ignore the pinch in my heart.

The sun rose higher and the birds sang. I thought, what a strange summer this has been. Not yet ten o'clock, and the light was blazing. The garden looks different to when we arrived, bleached brown and yellow by all the sun, and we are different too, I suppose. But the birds still sing, and the stream still rushes by, even if it is lower than it was. The rowan tree still shades the edge of the paddock and the moor stretches out around us.

'Some things are inevitable,' Mum said yesterday, talking about the house. But I don't want them to be.

The Film Diaries of Bluebell Gadsby

Scene Seventeen
Grandma

INTERIOR. DAY.

Bright light filters round the edges
of the drawn curtains fluttering at
the open windows, but the overall
impression of GRANDMA's room is of
stillness and shadow. Camera zooms
in, lingering over details - a bowl
of white roses on the dressing
table; an otter roughly carved in
wood on the mantelpiece; photographs
in silver frames - Grandma in her
wedding dress on the steps of a London
church, smiling at her father before
going in; holding Dad as a baby in
his christening robes; Grandma and

Grandpa in holiday clothes, in front of some ruins in Greece; Grandpa receiving an award; Mr Pigeon and some sheep in front of the brand-new Land Rover.

The bed has been imperfectly made, but the sheets are more or less straight, the blanket smooth. In the centre of the bed, propped against plump white pillows, Grandma sleeps. Her head is tilted back. Every now and then she gives a tiny snore, the only indication that she is actually breathing. The cut on her forehead is livid against her pale skin, which looks even paler, somehow, against the white of the pillow. She does not look like Grandma at all.

She looks like the people on that hospital ward.

Elsie lies beside the bed, head resting on her paws, watching. CAMERAMAN (BLUEBELL) takes a step forward. Elsie growls. Grandma stirs and opens her eyes.

                    GRANDMA
                     Blue?

Cameraman does not answer.

                    GRANDMA
          Blue, darling, are you crying?

                   CAMERAMAN
                      No.

                    GRANDMA
             What are you filming?

                   CAMERAMAN
                  Everything.

An estate agent came today. That's where Mum and Dad went yesterday in the car, to see her. She came halfway through the morning, as we were preparing to go to the river at Tarby. Mum was bouncing Pumpkin's pram to try and get him to sleep, and Twig was arguing with her that it was perfectly fine for him to cycle with a twisted ankle.

'Because there is no pressure,' Twig explained. 'Then when we get to where we leave the bikes, I will use the crutches. I can strap them to the rack, like French people do with bread. Swimming will be good for it. Tell her, Skye.'

'Why me?'

'You're always hurting yourself.'

I knew at once what she was. Who wears a navy suit on a blazing hot day to visit a house in the middle of the country? She gushed from the moment she stepped out of her smart little silver car.

'I love it!' she cried, and 'It's exactly how you described!'

'You can go now, kids,' Dad said.

'Even me?' Twig asked.

Dad said that Twig had been extremely convincing and that the beneficial effects of cycling, walking and river-swimming on twisted ankles were not to be underestimated.

Jas said, 'Who is she?'

The estate agent lady produced a clipboard and one of those electronic tape measures and said, 'Shall we get started?'

I said, 'I think we should stay.'

Twig sighed. Jas said, 'Fine, but in that case I get to look after Pumpkin.'

The four of us sat on the bench and watched Mum and Dad and the lady (whose name is Yvonne) walk all around the garden, the length of the drive, then down towards the paddock and the barn. A white butterfly drifted past and settled on the edge of Pumpkin's pram. He cooed and tried to grab it. It flew off.

'A sign of luck,' Jas said, but Skye pulled a face at me.

It would take a lot more than a butterfly to save Horsehill.

'Wonderful roses,' we heard Yvonne say as they came back past us towards the house.

'The field beyond the paddock is also ours,' Dad said. 'There's plenty of land to build on, and of course there's the old barn which could be converted.'

'Do you know who she is?' Jas asked.

They did not take the news well. The minute Yvonne left, they set on Dad.

'You can't sell Horsehill!' Twig was outraged. 'It's our home!'

'What about the ponies?' Jas cried. 'What about *Grandma*?'

Dad said he was very sad and sorry too, but that Grandma agreed it was for the best.

'She *agrees*?' Twig was outraged.

'I won't let you!' Jas vowed. 'I'll chain myself to the house! I'll tie myself to a tree! I'll lock myself in and never come out!'

Dad said they were being ridiculous. Jas told him she hated him. Dad lost his temper.

'Just look at the state of the place!' he shouted.

We looked. There was the garden, with its roses and fruit trees and potager. The lovely moor. The bridge over the stream, and the friendly house in its coppice of trees.

'The paths,' Dad said. 'The windows. The damp. Go inside and see what I'm talking about.'

And so we looked some more, and this time we saw it as he does. The weeds choking the paths, and the cracked, loose paving stones outside the kitchen. The ivy creeping in through cracks in the walls of the boot room, and the paint peeling off the windowsills, the gutter hanging at an angle beneath Grandma's bedroom and the damp spreading in dark corners of the hall, the peeling wallpaper in the dining room where nobody goes and the carpet curling off the stairs. Dad marched us through the house pointing everything out and I thought, Horsehill is like Grandma, it suddenly grew old.

Twig told Dad he had spoilt everything.

'I am just trying to show you things as they really are.' Dad ran his hands through his hair. 'I don't like this any more than you do.'

'Don't do it then,' Jas said, and Dad left, muttering about kids who didn't understand a thing and sounding a bit like Zoran.

'I'm going to the stream,' Jas said. Twig picked up his crutches and said he'd go with her. I followed with Skye and we all sat on the bridge with our feet dangling over the water.

'We have to do something,' Twig said.

Jas said, 'But what?'

That's the question.

Today I learned to ride without a saddle.

'But I don't want to,' I told Skye when he suggested it.

'There's nothing to be scared of,' he said.

'I'm not *scared*, I'm just not interested,' I explained, but I don't think it's possible for Skye to understand people not being interested in every aspect of horses.

Ponies are more slippery than you expect, and even when they are as fat as Hester their backbones are still hard and not at all comfortable to sit on. It was fine as long as we were just walking, but then Jas said that we had to trot and suddenly I was being thrown about with my arms and legs and even my head flying all over the place, until I finally bounced right off Hester and into a patch of grass containing at least three stinging nettles, a thistle, an anthill and some horse droppings.

When I stopped seeing stars, I noticed Skye was crying.

Seriously, real tears. Of flipping laughter.

And here's the thing. Even though I shouted at him that it wasn't funny. Even though I stomped off that field with my nose in the air and horse poo all over my jeans, and was only nice to him again after he let me push him in the stream, even though he made Twig film the whole thing and MY ENTIRE FAMILY still cry with laughter every time they watch it, I'm glad he's here.

This evening after dinner the two of us climbed the oak tree. Last time I went all the way to the top,

I was terrified. I only did it to prove I could to Iris. I've grown since then, which makes tree climbing easier in one way, because I can reach further, but more difficult too, because I'm heavier and the branches bend further under my weight. We didn't talk much as we climbed, except to tell each other where to put our hands and feet, but when we got to the top we dared each other to look out over the highest branches. And as we stood there, with our arms and legs all scratched and our hair full of twigs and leaves, the tree swayed in the breeze like a ship on the open sea, and the moon fell on our faces, and I thought again how Skye at Horsehill feels absolutely right.

They can't sell it. They just can't.

Friday 22 August

Flora called again, and complained because I took too long to answer.

'It's not even seven o'clock!' I protested.

'I have jet lag,' she said, like that was a reason for waking everyone else up. 'Things are hotting up on the South American front. Gloria has found a buyer for the stables, and she has entered negotiations with some Argentinian gauchos. They are coming to interview her tomorrow. Why is Zoran not here yet?'

'You are going to have to do something pretty spectacular,' I told Zoran at breakfast. We've brought a table in from the garden, and even though it's a bit small and still dirty despite a lot of washing, it means if we squeeze up we can all sit together again to eat.

'Why does Zoran have to be spectacular?' Jas asked.

'Don't put the spoon back in the jam after you've licked it,' I said.

'Gloria is running away to South America,' Twig told her.

Jas said, 'Gloria's leaving as well?' and burst into tears. Dad came in and asked what was going on and who the hell called so early this morning.

'It was Flora,' I said. 'Zoran has commitment issues and won't move in with Gloria and now she's emigrating to Argentina.'

'I do *not* have commitment issues,' Zoran protested.

'I don't really understand what is going on,' Dad said. 'But if Gloria was my girlfriend and threatening to leave the country, I would be hot-footing it back to London.'

'Gloria's lovely,' Twig agreed. 'Even if she is a little scary.'

'She's wonderful!' Jas cried.

'You're running out of time,' I told Zoran.

He looked dazed, like he was only just beginning to wake up.

'You're right,' he said. 'I'd better go and pack.'

I made more tea and took it up to Grandma with some toast. She was sitting up in bed, reading *Les Misérables*.

'This is excellent stuff,' she said. 'I can't understand why Twig stopped reading it.'

'He's moved on to higher things,' I said. 'Like gardening and wildlife. You look better.'

'I feel it.'

I wandered round her room as she ate, looking at all her things.

'I suppose your father has told you about the house,' she said. 'That's why you were in here the other day, filming everything and crying.'

'We're all furious with him,' I said.

'Well don't be. It's not easy for him either.'

'But then why is he making you leave?'

'Nobody *makes* me do anything,' said Grandma.

'An estate agent came,' I told her. 'Dad showed her the field. He said there was plenty of land to build on, and also that the barn could be converted.'

'Bathtubs falling through the ceiling!' Grandma murmured. 'Starlit car crashes on the moor, escaping from hospital, ranting like a lunatic! None of these things are normal, Blue.'

'You're just still upset because of nearly killing Twig.'

'I'm not upset, I'm old.' Grandma leaned back into her pillow and closed her eyes. 'A nice sensible flat, like your father says. That will be much better for me.'

'What about us?' I asked.

She opened her eyes again. 'What about you?'

'How will we come and visit, in your sensible flat?'

'I imagine it will have a nice spare room or two. Why are you looking at me like that, like you would like to murder me?'

'Because it's not just about me,' I retorted. 'What about Skye and Lizzie? They love it here, especially Skye. And Zoran – how will he play the piano if you sell Horsehill?'

'Zoran can have the piano, if he wants it.'

'Where on earth would Zoran keep a huge grand piano?'

'I have to do what is right for me,' Grandma said.

'But we love it here.'

Grandma sighed in that way grown-ups do when they've decided you can't possibly understand them.

'Things change. Circumstances. I've told you before.'

'That was a completely different conversation. This is your home. It's who you are.'

'There's more to me than where I live, Blue.'

She tried to stop me going, but I didn't want to talk to her any more. 'You're just giving up,' I told her, and stormed out of the room.

She was standing by her window when I reached the far end of the garden. I looked up and saw her watching me. In her white nightdress, with her silver hair brushed out over her shoulders, she looked like one of Grandpa's ghosts. The ghost of Horsehill, refusing to leave. Except that she is leaving.

I walked for ages out on the moor, and there were more ghosts there. Grandpa and my great-grandparents. Elsie and Mr Pigeon. Flora and me, riding out together two winters ago when we came at half-term. The four of us, trekking across country on walks, Mum and Dad when we were little, before they stopped coming after Iris died, when they couldn't bear to remember how she was here – always climbing, always running, always splashing in and out of water.

Everywhere I go here, I meet the ghost of Iris, but today she wasn't alone. I came to Grandma's cairn and there was another child with her, and though I couldn't see his face, I knew that it was Pumpkin. I sat down by a tiny stream and cooled my hands and feet and face, and I could feel them sitting right beside me.

'So what are you going to do?' Iris asked.

'What can I do?' I replied. 'They've decided.'

'Pfff!' Iris said. 'Grown-ups!'

As I walked back towards home, the ghost of Iris and the future Pumpkin melted away and the moor became just a moor again, wild and sweet and beautiful, but they left behind the germ of an idea. And I know it was a good one, because when I got home the others had all had it too, and I could see the excitement on their faces.

'Zoran's gone,' Twig told me. 'But we've spoken to Flora, and we've talked to Grandma, and we've got a plan.'

The Film Diaries of Bluebell Gadsby

Scene Eighteen
Back to the Barn

EXTERIOR *AND* INTERIOR. DAY.

SKYE, JASMINE, FATHER, MOTHER, PUMPKIN
(in his pram), TWIG (on crutches),
GRANDMA (fully dressed, walking very
slowly leaning on Skye's arm) and
CAMERAMAN (BLUE) stand before the
barn. It is mid-afternoon, and hot,
though the sky has turned from blue
to grey and the air feels different
today - close and clammy, like it
might even rain. Elsie lies in the
long grass beneath the brambles on the
edge of the path Skye and Twig have
hacked out, chewing a piece of wood.

Twig holds the key, but now that

302

they are all here, he hesitates to use
it.

                    GRANDMA
            (wiping sweat from her brow)
        Hurry up, dear, before we all melt.

                    FATHER
        Mother, I really do think you
        should be in bed. Also, would someone
        mind telling me what we are all
                    doing here?

                    TWIG
        I am a little worried about the bats.

                    ALL
                JUST OPEN THE DOOR!

Twig obeys. The door swings open. All
peer in. There is no sign of bats. All
enter. The barn appears exactly as it
was before: dusty, cobwebby and very,
very full.

MOTHER

What a wonderful space!

FATHER

I am still waiting for
an explanation.

Still leaning on Skye, Grandma wanders
further into the barn, pokes her
stick at rubber tyres, peers into the
feeding troughs full of junk, runs her
fingers along the ancient plough and
turns to beam at the camera.

GRANDMA

I think this is going to be perfectly
splendid. David dear, perhaps you
and Cassie could take me back to the
house? I will explain everything
as we walk.

Grandma, Mum and Dad leave. Twig,
Jasmine and Skye sit on a pile of
tyres, looking discouraged.

SKYE

Must you film?

CAMERAMAN

I'm doing a before and after. Start!

I promise to help once you get going.

JASMINE

(looking very small)

This place is huge. We have just over

twenty-four hours, if we don't sleep.

There are three of us. Five, if Mum

and Dad help. Five and a half, if you

count Twig and his crutches.

Skye stands, pulls a tyre from its
pile, flips it onto its side and rolls
it out of the barn. He returns to do
the same with the next one, pushes his
hair off his glasses, smearing oil and
dust over his face. Jasmine does the
same. Twig limps to the wheelbarrow,
pushes it to the stalls and begins
to throw in junk. Skye glares at the
camera.

SKYE

Put the camera down, Bluebell.

CAMERAMAN

Listen! Someone's coming.

Outside, Elsie barks. All pause and
listen. A woman's voice calls Skye's
name.

SKYE

Mum's back!

Elsie's barking intensifies. Lizzie
appears in the doorway.

LIZZIE

There you are! Look who I found
waiting when I got home!

A tall, bearded man steps into the
barn behind her. Skye drops his tyre
and runs to hug him.

Not a lot got done for a while after Skye's parents arrived.

'I missed you both too much!' As well as being very large and bearded, Skye's father has a very loud laugh and a voice stronger even than Grandma's before she got sick. Also, unlike Skye and Lizzie, quite a strong French accent. 'So I thought, to hell with this teaching job! I found someone to step in for me, leaped into the car and drove over to surprise you. But there was nobody home! I didn't know you were all away!'

'You've found us now!' Lizzie beamed and he showered her upturned face with kisses. I literally mean that. *Showered.* We all had to look away.

'I brought cake!' Lizzie cried when the kissing stopped. 'Who wants tea?'

'We have work to do,' Jas informed her.

'We're emptying the barn,' Twig explained.

Lizzie looked mystified and asked why, but Isambard roared with laughter like he thought Jas and Twig were the funniest thing ever and said that once he'd had cake and tea, he would help.

'It's coffee and walnut,' Lizzie said. 'With proper glacé icing. And everyone, more lovely news! Ollie is up at the house. I brought him back with me. Isn't that another lovely surprise?'

My heart skipped a beat.

I glanced at Skye, but he was staring at the floor, drawing circles with his trainer in the dust.

Jas tugged at my sleeve.

'He's a little bit scary.' She pointed, not very discreetly, at Isambard. 'But coffee and walnut is my absolute favourite.'

Twig groaned and said how were we ever going to finish if we never even started?

'Please come with me,' Jas whispered.

Twig stayed. Jas and I followed Skye and his parents towards the house. She chattered all the way up. I didn't hear a word she said.

Ollie was sitting on the front doorstep, bouncing a small rubber ball. Jas pulled at my hand, but I told her to go in without me.

He looked up. He smiled. And my heart skipped beat after beat.

'You didn't say goodbye,' I said.

'That's why I came back.'

I sat down next to him on the step.

'Skye told me about your parents. I'm so sorry.'

'Thanks, Blue.'

He took my hand.

And it felt nothing like holding Skye's hand up on Satan's Tor. That was friendly, and comforting, and kind. This was . . .

This felt like electricity.

I didn't care that he hadn't told me the truth about his parents. That he left without saying goodbye. That I hadn't heard a word from him since.

'You're not wearing my necklace,' he said.

He was upset. That explained everything.

I reached up and touched Skye's pendant.

'It's just that it's an iris,' I said.

I didn't even care that he didn't seem to understand.

'Blue!' Jas appeared at the door, her face full of cake. 'Don't you want any?'

I laughed. I felt giddy.

'I'm going to get some cake for Twig,' I said. 'He's down at the barn. Will you come with us?'

'I'll wait for you here.'

In the kitchen, everyone was crammed around the old garden table, and Dad was looking dazed.

'Have you told them?' I asked.

'I think it's a marvellous idea,' Mum said.

'It's insane,' Dad said. 'That's what it is.'

'Cassie's right,' Grandma chided. 'It's positively brilliant.'

I cut two slices of cake, wrapped them in kitchen roll, poured out two mugs of tea, put it all on a tray and said that I was going back to the barn.

'We will be right behind you!' Isambard Hanratty announced, tucking into more tea.

Ollie wasn't on the front step any more. I went down to the barn. Twig must have found a way of rolling tyres despite his bad foot, because there were more lying at the entrance to the barn. I stopped to stack them up then paused. Someone was talking.

Ollie.

'I heard about your midnight disaster,' Ollie said. 'How your gran had to come and rescue you.'

Twig didn't answer.

'With your sisters,' Ollie said. 'Dude! Rescued by a bunch of girls.'

Twig mumbled something.

'*Ooh, I'm scared of the witch! Ooh, I have to be rescued by my Grandma!*' Ollie started to laugh. 'Man, you're a loser.'

I stepped quietly into the barn. The boys didn't even turn.

In my mind, Twig had been lying on the ground, clutching his ankle and crying fat tears, but in real life it wasn't like that at all.

Crutch under one arm, sweat-stiffened hair standing on end, clothes smeared with dirt and cobwebs, Twig was advancing on Ollie – limping, yes, but also brandishing an ancient agricultural implement.

'Shut up! Shut up! Shut up!' Twig shouted. He jabbed the implement at Ollie, who ducked.

'What the . . .' Ollie cried.

Twig jabbed at him again. Ollie stumbled backwards and fell to the floor. Twig stood above him, holding the implement like it was a sword and he was a medieval servant.

'I am not a loser!' Twig yelled. 'I AM MY FATHER'S ONLY ELDEST SON!'

Ollie rolled into a ball and covered his head. Twig carried on jabbing. I ran in and caught his arm.

'Jesus!'' Ollie said. 'Did you see that? He's insane.'

'Stop it!' I shouted at him. 'Just stop it!'

'Me?'

'Yes, you! Twig, put that thing away. Go and . . . go and get some cake or something.'

'I'm not leaving you with this creep,' Twig said.

'Please.'

He limped to the door, and then Ollie and I were alone.

'Iris was my *sister*.' I was shaking so badly I thought my legs wouldn't hold me, but I couldn't sit down. Not to say what I had to say.

What I had to say, I wanted to shout from the rooftops.

Iris was my sister. That never goes away. If you don't get that, you don't get me.

And you don't talk to my family like that. Not one of them. Not ever.

But shouting's never been my style.

'I was only teasing him,' Ollie said.

'It wasn't funny.'

Making people feel small. Laughing at them. Lying to them. Behaving like they don't matter, like feelings can just be picked up and thrown away like rubbish.

These are all things you can't do.

However unhappy you are. However bad you feel.

However heart-breakingly beautiful you are.

Ollie shifted his weight from one foot to another, and back again. 'Come on, Blue.'

'I liked you,' I said. 'I really, really liked you. But all summer, it's been about you. It's always been about you. I don't care that your parents are getting divorced or that your father's had an affair. It doesn't mean you can treat people badly. Skye's been miserable too, but he's kind to people. He's worth a thousand of you. I don't like you any more at all, in fact I think I . . .'

'That's enough, Blue.'

Lizzie had appeared beside me, and Ollie was crying. Real, proper tears, like that day we saw him in the car park in Plumpton.

He wasn't handsome any more. He didn't make my heart skip. He was just a boy, as lost and bewildered as the rest of us by the changes life had thrown at him.

'That's enough,' Lizzie repeated. 'Unless I'm very much mistaken, we have a barn to clear.'

Skye, Jas, Twig, Ollie, me. Lizzie, Zoran, Grandma. This summer that we shared was something different for everyone. It was about Ollie's parents separating and Grandma growing old, about Zoran loving Gloria and Skye finding his place, about all of us welcoming Pumpkin. It was about all of us shifting up to make room for the things that changed, as one of us grew old and another took over our lives, as some went away and others arrived.

People come and people go. You've just got to learn to make room for them.

We worked hard today. All of us. Those of us who have been here all summer and those who had just arrived. Dad, grumbling that it would never work. Mum whenever Pumpkin was asleep, and Isambard harder than anyone, and even Grandma, who kept on making coffee and sandwiches late into the night when she should have been in bed – when we should *all* have been asleep.

This has to work – for all of us.

It's gone three o'clock now. The barn is almost empty – the lower part, that is. No one dared go up to the bats' platform, and the top window has remained firmly shut all afternoon. Everything that can be burned has been wheeled to a corner of the field, stacked up for a bonfire. The tyres are in the paddock, along with the rusty old car and the plough – Jas says she has plans for them, but won't say what. Everything we can't burn is out of sight behind the barn. Isambard, who drives a truck that makes the Land Rover look like a mini ('It's for my artwork!' he protested when Grandma told him it was a monster. 'I use *really big* canvases!') is going to drive it all to the dump.

Twig says we have to be up and working again by seven at the latest. Tomorrow – which is actually later today – we have cleaning to do. The barn must be swept, the mangers filled, hay nets put up. The field must be fenced, the paddock mown, signs must be painted. Marigold and Hester must be brushed to within an inch of their lives. I don't know how Flora has done it, but she says that she and Zach, Zoran and Gloria will be here just after tea-time.

The Film Diaries of Bluebell Gadsby

Scene Nineteen
The Horsehill
School of Riding

DAYTIME. EXTERIOR.

At the sound of GLORIA's car turning
off the road, the many occupants of
Horsehill (who had all been enjoying
a much deserved tea break) burst into
action and assume their positions.
CAMERAMAN (BLUEBELL) films from a
distance, hidden by a rosebush.

The car stops. Gloria and ZORAN step
out of the front. A grungy-looking
boy with hair in his eyes and lots
of leather bracelets spills out of
the back, carrying a guitar - ZACH.
FLORA emerges last. She wears very

short hot-pants, riding boots and a horseshoe-print T-shirt in honour of the occasion. She looks very pleased with herself. She shades her eyes, making a big show of looking for her family, then guides Gloria and Zoran towards the paddock. Zach follows, his guitar strapped round his neck, strumming Elton John's 'Live Like Horses'.

In the paddock SKYE, armed with a whip, stands in the centre of a ring made of rubber tyres bellowing orders which JASMINE on HESTER struggles to execute because she is giggling so much. The brambles which choked the path down to the barn have gone, mown down this morning by Skye and ISAMBARD. Nothing stands now between the barn and the paddock but the old rowan tree, casting its shadow onto a makeshift courtyard. The ground is ragged but it has been raked and swept. Twig, Ollie and Dad sit on a bench in front of the barn, polishing tack, while Isambard leads MARIGOLD around the courtyard with MOTHER (once a keen horsewoman herself) on her back, clutching an ecstatic PUMPKIN. LIZZIE, for want of anything else to do, is sweeping. In the far corner of the courtyard, the rusted 1940s Morris Minor convertible bursts with pots of scarlet geraniums.

GRANDMA stands before the door to the barn. Multi-coloured party balloons float behind her, tied to the ancient hand-plough. She looks nervous. Flora, Gloria and Zoran stop before her and she steps aside to reveal a sign reading WELCOME TO THE HORSEHILL SCHOOL OF RIDING.

GLORIA
I don't understand.

GRANDMA
Let me show you.

Together, they step into the barn. Mother and Pumpkin dismount. Jasmine and Skye come in from the paddock.

The others abandon their posts. All follow Grandma, Zoran and Gloria into the barn.

The floor has been swept. The cobwebs are gone. The bats keep their distance. Around the edges of the barn, twelve individual stalls gleam. Above each stall, on bits of coloured card, are the names of every single one of Gloria's London horses (at Jas's request, in case she decides to bring them). There are balloons everywhere. Also, streamers, confetti and more geraniums. Zach does a spontaneous riff on 'Oh Happy Day' on his guitar.

JASMINE
(no longer able to contain
her excitement)
WE MADE YOU A RIDING SCHOOL! YOU CAN LIVE HERE WITH ZORAN AND GRANDMA!!!

All beam as they gaze at Gloria, waiting for her to speak. Twig sucks a splinter out of his finger. Skye rubs the blister on his thumb. Isambard

has a slight squint, the result of
an unfortunate encounter last night
with one of the ancient agricultural
implements.

Surely Gloria cannot fail to
appreciate the fruit of their hard
work?

'But I don't understand,' Gloria said.

'You and Zoran can live here with Grandma!' Twig said. 'We cleared the barn and arranged the paddock specially for you. You can move your stables here when you sell them!'

'Zoran loves it here, and he could play the piano and compose and maybe teach,' I added. 'That way you both get what you want, and Grandma doesn't have to move.'

Even as I said it, I could see there was a major flaw in the plan. At this stage, Gloria was meant to be laughing and hugging and thanking everyone.

'You knew,' she said to Zoran.

'I wanted to surprise you,' he said, and I could tell he could see the flaw too.

'But I don't *want* to live here,' Gloria said. She turned to look at us all. 'I'm sorry. It's sweet and everything, but you can't just tell people how to live their lives.'

There was total silence in the barn as she walked back towards the door. At the entrance, she turned and said, 'I'd like to speak to Zoran in private, please. Then I'm going back to London. There are people waiting to see me there, and it's important.'

She stopped in front of Flora.

'You played me,' she said.

'No more than you played Zoran,' Flora replied.

Gloria left. Zoran hurried after her. Jas tried to go too, but Grandma held her back.

'She's right, of course,' Isambard pronounced. 'People must make their own choices.'

'But it was such a *good* choice,' Jas argued.

'It was a wonderful idea,' Grandma sighed.

'I thought so,' said Mum.

I don't think I have ever seen so many people look so dejected.

'I told you it was crazy,' Dad said, but he looked dejected too.

Everyone went off their separate ways after that. Isambard said he might as well start taking stuff to the dump. Ollie and Skye and Dad offered to help. Zach and Flora wandered off hand in hand towards the stream. Grandma went to take a nap in her deckchair, Twig climbed the oak tree to read, and Mum and Lizzie took Pumpkin off for a walk in his pushchair. Mum asked Jas if she wanted to go with them, but Jas said she was too depressed even for Pumpkin, and walked back to the house with me.

'All summer I have been longing for him to be

here,' she sighed. 'And now that he is, it's like it doesn't even matter. Why?'

'Other things seem more important, I guess.'

'At least he's seen it,' Jas said. 'I mean, I don't think he'll remember it, but at least he will have been here. That's something, isn't it?'

We stopped at the kitchen door. Someone had left a basket of tomatoes on the step. There was a box of eggs there too from Lizzie, along with one of Elsie's chewed-up logs.

'The roses need deadheading,' I said.

'It's the most beautiful place I have ever known,' Jas whispered. 'I will never, ever forget it.'

'Let's go and get our swimming things,' I suggested. 'Then go and meet Mum and take Pumpkin to the stream. You can hold him and I'll film it, and when he's old enough we'll show him when he swam in a river for the very first time.'

'There's hardly any water any more.'

'There's enough left for him.'

Gloria and Zoran were in the living room when I came back downstairs. I didn't mean to listen. Just, the door was partly open.

'It's all about them again,' Gloria said. 'This grand solution for us. It's actually to help them.'

'No,' Zoran said. 'No, no, no, no, no.'

'What is it then? How is *this* the right solution for *me*?'

There was a long pause. Zoran started fingering the piano. He was only playing with one hand, but I recognised the opening notes of his sonata. 'It was the children's idea,' he admitted. 'But when they called to tell me about it, on my way back to London, I thought if you could just see . . .'

'See what?'

'The possibilities. Oh, I know it's not Argentina and the pampas and everything you've dreamed of, but . . .'

He played some more, one note at a time.

'But?' Gloria prompted.

Zoran sighed. 'We were made for different things, you and I,' he said. 'You were made for being outside, for horses and big horizons and adventure. I was made for music, and for looking after people. I'm not trying to sound like a saint when I say that, but I'm *good* at it, Gloria. I'm good at looking after people.'

'But where does that leave *us*?'

More sonata. More silence. I had to strain forward to hear what Zoran said next.

'We were made for different things,' he said. 'But

we were also made for each other. We were, Gloria. I love you. Let me look after you, too.'

I peeped through the crack in the door. Zoran was leaning against the piano. Gloria stood in front of the window, looking out.

'It *is* beautiful,' she sighed. 'But Zoran, they aren't family. We would have no status, no rights . . .'

'There would be a contract. And they are like family to me.'

'Living on top of each other . . .'

'The house is big. The stables would be your domain. We would have our own rooms. I assure you, Constance is still a very independent woman.'

'But how long will she remain independent?'

'Who knows? It's worth a punt, isn't it?'

He was playing with two hands now, and Gloria finally paid attention.

'That tune. It was Dad's favourite.'

One-fingered, Zoran picked out the melody.

'Play the whole thing.'

And Zoran played like I have never heard him play before. It started quietly and just grew and grew, until it felt like there was nothing in the house but music. No, it felt like the house *was* music, and not just the house but me, too. It felt like everything I am was captured in the way Zoran played this afternoon, and in the silence that followed, everything was different.

'Please don't go to Argentina, Gloria,' Zoran said. 'It's so very far away.'

'One more time,' she said, and Zoran played again.

'I thought I was writing it to show you how much music means to me,' he told her when he finished. 'But all the time, I was writing it for you.'

'For me?'

'If you'll have it. Gloria, will you marry me?'

I didn't tell a soul what happened, but the living room has two doors, and they are both excellent for eavesdropping. By the time I found Jas again, everyone knew that Gloria had changed her mind, that she and Zoran were staying and that they were getting married.

Later, I sat by the stream with Flora, watching Jas and Twig dangle Pumpkin in the water with Mum looking anxious and hovering behind them. Zach lay on the river bank, playing 'It's Such a Perfect Day'.

'What did Gloria mean, you played her?' I asked.

'That I lied to get her here, I guess. I couldn't exactly tell her the truth.'

'What did you tell her? And what did you mean, she played Zoran?'

Flora grinned. 'Promise you won't tell? There is no buyer for the stables, and there is no job in Argentina. She made the whole thing up to kick Zoran's butt and get him back to London. It was Zach who rumbled her. He's been to Argentina, and he asked her where she was going, and she couldn't say. I agreed not to tell Zoran and played along to help her out. Then you guys had your idea, so I made her come back here. I said the whole Argentina thing would be way more convincing if she agreed to come and say goodbye.'

'And she was all right with that?'

'Zach helped. He said Zoran would only love her more if she did.'

'But that's so devious!'

'I know!' I've never seen Flora look so smug.

'That sounds like a very high-risk strategy,' I said. 'All those lies!'

'Oh don't be so sensible,' Flora said.

I am *not* sensible, I wanted to tell her. In the past four weeks, I have jumped off a very high bridge, and ridden out twice at dawn to watch the sunrise from the steepest outcrop on the whole of Dartmoor, and I have kidnapped my grandmother from hospital and sort of almost fallen in love with a boy who never loved me back. But then I thought of Zoran again, what he said about his own sister, how in the eyes of our family, we never really change.

I am what I am. It doesn't matter what other people think.

Sunday 24 August

Storm clouds gathered all evening and in the hot still air it grew difficult to breathe, but that didn't stop us. Isambard lit the bonfire, Dad drove into Plumpton for supplies, Mum and Lizzie and Zoran and Grandma cooked, Jas and Skye showed Gloria every inch of the new stables.

Flora tried to make me dress up for the party.

'Those two boys,' she said. 'Both so cute.'

'I don't want to.'

'You can borrow anything you want.' She emptied her bag over her bed. It's amazing how many different clothes one person can have. Sequins and dresses and crop tops. Scarves, mini-skirts, dungarees. 'Anything you like!' Flora implored. 'Just not your jeans and flip-flops.'

'This,' I said, holding up a cornflower blue T-shirt.

'I use that to sleep in!'

'This,' I insisted. 'And your make-up bag.'

She wanted to help me, but I wouldn't let her. I took her bag into the bathroom, which I suppose isn't really a bathroom at the moment as it still doesn't have a bath, and I looked at myself in the mirror, and I thought about that day, ages ago, when I came back pink and sweaty from our first expedition with Skye and Ollie to Melisandra's pool, and how much I hated how I looked. I took Grandma's hairbrush and brushed my hair so it was sleek and shiny, with the fringe hanging just over my eyes and the back hanging in two loose plaits over my shoulders, tied with little scraps of ribbon. I used Flora's powder to take the shine off my nose, and a bit of eyeliner and quite a lot of mascara to make my eyes bigger, and a touch of her purple lipstick just to see what it looked like (nice). I found my nicest jeans, the tight ones that make my legs look longer, slipped on the T-shirt and fastened Skye's iris round my neck, and then I looked at myself in the mirror and I liked how I looked.

Isambard also has a guitar. He brought it to the party. He and Zach played. Flora sang with them. Zoran and Gloria danced, barefoot, laughing.

Grandma sat in her deckchair with Elsie at her feet, keeping time with her stick.

Mum and Dad held hands.

Jas announced she was going to read her epic poem. Twig snatched it out of her hands. 'To hell with literature!' he shouted, and threw *Les Misérables* in the fire.

Mum retrieved Jas's poem before he burned that too and promised that tomorrow Jas could read the whole thing out to all of us.

'When it's nice and quiet,' she said.

Jas stuffed the poem into Pumpkin's pram and vanished towards the paddock.

All the grown-ups drank too much.

On the stroke of midnight, Jas cantered into the field on Hester, and Grandma found her hat at last.

'What have you done to it?' she cried.

'It's for their honeymoon!' Jas shouted, except I'm not sure anyone heard her because they were laughing so much. Jas slid off Hester's back and led her over to the fire for Gloria to admire her in her bonnet. Hester bolted. Gloria, Isambard, Flora and Zach sprinted after her. The hat flew into the fire to burn alongside Victor Hugo.

'What about my cashmere cardigan?' Grandma demanded, but I haven't dared tell her yet.

Ollie sidled up to me by the fire as I tried to pull the hat out.

'I've been trying to talk to you all night,' he said. 'I'm leaving tomorrow. For good, this time. I just wanted to say I'm sorry.'

'Are you going to be OK?'

'I guess so. I want to live with Mum. I don't think I can face this new woman of Dad's. Not yet, anyway.'

'You can always come here,' I told him. 'In the holidays. We'll be coming a lot more from now on.'

He hesitated. 'I do like you, Blue.'

'Thanks,' I said. 'I liked you too.'

'Past tense,' he said.

'Yeah. Past tense.'

And I knew we'd never see Ollie at Horsehill again.

Skye was standing on the edge of the field with Elsie, just out of range of the firelight.

'Come on,' I said.

'Where?'

'You'll see.'

I did think we might get lost on the moor. Memories of Grandpa's stories played through my mind, of bodies being discovered decades after they'd strayed off paths and drowned. But I found the tiny tributary soon enough, and together Skye and I picked our way carefully across country.

I pulled two stones out of my pocket when we reached the cairn.

'One each,' I told him.

'What do we do with them?'

'We add them to the cairn. We don't make a wish, exactly. We just – think of something, I suppose. Like a kind of tribute.'

We balanced our stones in with the others, and stood not talking for a moment.

'What did you think about?' he asked.

'My family,' I said. 'All of them. You?'

'Same,' he said. 'But also friends who feel like family.'

We started to walk back. 'Did you know Gloria's offered me a job?' he said. 'A proper one, every day after school, and weekends.'

Winter, short days, school. Skye here, and us in London, and people coming for lessons, people who know nothing about any of us. Horsehill saved but no longer ours. I never thought before how strange that would be.

'There'll be loads of little girls coming for Pony Club,' I said. 'They'll all fall in love with you. Pony Club girls always fall in love with stable hands.'

Skye looked appalled.

'You'll make loads of friends,' I told him.

We stopped on the bridge. Thunder rumbled overhead. A few fat raindrops fell, making circles in the stream. I shivered. Skye took off his hoody and put it round my shoulders, then stood with his arm around me.

It was nice. Not exciting. Not boyfriend-like at all. Just friends. Maybe even soul mates.

He pulled at my plaits.

'I like your hair like this,' he said. 'It makes you look like you.'

'I have layers,' I informed him. 'Lots of them. Under this schoolgirl exterior, I am a mysterious and magical creature.'

'Girls are so weird,' he said.

We stood there for ages, with our arms round each other. Zach started playing his guitar by the bonfire in the field, and the others sang along with him. Elsie splashed about in the stream beneath us, doing whatever spaniels do in water – sniffing, searching, hunting out prey. We stood and we listened and we held each other and as the rain came down harder the circles in the water grew bigger and bigger and broke into other circles in a sort of elaborate, geometric dance that only broke when Elsie bounced out from under the bridge. And then we ran with her, slipping and sliding on the wet grass until Flora's cornflower blue T-shirt was soaked through and my make-up was gone and my sleek hair had turned to rats' tails. We held hands and joined the others and danced around the bonfire in the rain, Ollie and Isambard and Lizzie and Skye, Zoran and Gloria and all my family, Grandma with her stick and Pumpkin in Mum's arms, and I tried not to mind that summer was nearly over.

The Film Diaries of Bluebell Gadsby

Scene Twenty:
All About Pumpkin

INTERIOR. JUST BEFORE DAWN.

The tiny room (more of a closet)
where babies at Horsehill have all
traditionally slept is full of light,
the result of PUMPKIN's parents
forgetting to pull the blind when they
put him to bed after the party.

For the first time in nearly a
month, the sky is a normal English
grey instead of blazing blue.

Pumpkin lies on his back in the
cot which has served generations of
Gadsby children, making those fretting
noises which directly precede out
and out, full-blown crying, but he is
momentarily silenced by the sight of

CAMERAMAN (BLUEBELL) as she balances her camera on the side of the cot.

From here on in, picture is somewhat disjointed.

                    CAMERAMAN
        Shh, you're going to wake the whole
                      house.

        DISEMBODIED VOICE OF JASMINE
        He wants his nappy changed. Get out
            of the way and I will do it.

                    CAMERAMAN
                  No, I will.

Much fumbling as Cameraman (who has never done this before) tries to remember how this works. The nappy, thankfully, is clean (if damp). Cameraman throws it in nearby bin and surveys Pumpkin who lies in splendid, carefree nakedness, regarding her with suspicion. Cameraman, drawing on a long-buried memory when Mother used to do it to Jasmine, blows air in

his face and down his tummy. Pumpkin
screws up his face.

                    CAMERAMAN
              He smiled at me!

                    JASMINE
         I wouldn't do that if I were you.

                    CAMERAMAN
              Don't be jealous.

A perfect arc of baby pee hits
Cameraman full in the face. Cameraman
screams. Jasmine explodes with
laughter. MOTHER appears, looking
anxious.

Pumpkin chortles. Just for a second,
a wicked expression crosses his face
which makes him look like someone
else, the sister he will never know.
Then, as his chortling dissolves
into happy gurgles, he becomes
unmistakeably himself.

If you enjoyed reading
All About Pumpkin,
read more by Natasha Farrant . . .

'Raucously funny.'
New York Times

"Funny
and poignant
with lots of heart"
The Bookseller

AFTER
IRIS

Natasha Farrant

Bluebell's life is chaotic: Mum and Dad are
always away, the new babysitter has no idea what
he's doing, and the whole family is trying to get
used to life without Iris.